CHARLOTTE PHILLIPS

I live in Wiltshire, UK, where I squash writing in between looking after my family, who have been taught not to notice that I'm rubbish at housework. I love watching American TV shows in my pyjamas and I can't live without coffee and cake.

Kiss Me on This Cold December Night

CHARLOTTE PHILLIPS

Harper*Impulse* an imprint of
HarperCollins*Publishers* Ltd
77–85 Fulham Palace Road
Hammersmith, London W6 8JB

www.harpercollins.co.uk

A Paperback Original 2014

First published in Great Britain in ebook format by Harper*Impulse* 2013

A catalogue record for this book
is available from the British Library

ISBN: 978-0-00-759169-5

Automatically produced by Atomik ePublisher from Easypress

For my lovely mum and dad. Mum, thanks for everything. And Dad, wherever you are, if it has internet access I know you'll be reading everything I write and forcing everyone else to do the same. Love you both.

CHAPTER ONE

'A suite if you have it, but I'll take anything.'

Tom Henley wrestled his credit card from his wallet. He might have had his plans thwarted by the bonkers British weather, which for some insane reason had decided to dump a shedload of snow over the entire country in late December, putting it bang on track for the first white Christmas in years, but that didn't mean he had to take it lying down.

'Odds on for a white Christmas,' the receptionist said, giving him a wink.

He stared at her beaming smile across the marble counter.

'And that would be a good thing because…?'

When you'd spent Christmas in Barbados every year for pretty much your entire life, snow was not something to be excited about. On the contrary, it was a *complication*. Christmas to him meant sunshine and white sandy beaches and swimming in the calm Caribbean sea. And family of course. Let's not forget that. This year, family responsibility would feature more than ever before. He pressed his thumb and finger to the bridge of his nose. The day had been on a steady nosedive since he'd attempted check in at Gatwick five hours ago only to be told that the entire place was at a standstill because of 'the wrong sort of snow.' Faced with the prospect of sleeping rough in the airport concourse, there was no way he was about to see it as a great adventure. A quick change of plan and now he was checking into the Lavington Hotel, his place to stay of choice whenever he came to London. Crystal chandeliers, velvet sofas, marble floors and freshly brewed coffee. Just what he needed after hours of airport tannoys, irritable crowds and fast food outlets. The relaxed luxury and familiarity of the place soothed him.

Or would do, if everyone would stop with the excitement over the UK's inability to cope with a bit of frozen water.

The receptionist's smile faltered.

'It's romantic, isn't it? Doesn't everyone always dream of a white Christmas? It's only a week away, I'm sure we'll hang onto the snow long enough for that. And it's really not that bad in London. The North has got the worst of it.'

Hang on to the snow? Oh just bloody *great*.

'I don't dream of a white Christmas,' he snapped. 'I've got commitments.'

'Work, is it?' Her tone had an edge of frost now that perfectly matched the weather.

'Work and family,' he snapped. The two things were going to be inseparable for him, more now than ever. 'The airport was at a standstill. It might not be too bad in London but apparently it's the wrong sort of snow. Whatever the hell that means. And there's some kind of issue with fog and visibility. In twelve hours I'm meant to be holding a glass of eggnog at the yearly family reunion and instead I'm stuck here for the foreseeable.'

Not that he had any particular sense of excitement about going. Anything lost its charm when you'd done it twenty-eight times. But of course the Christmas trip had nothing to do with his own excitement or his idea of what might constitute R and R. It was about duty and responsibility; had been for years now. And in his world those were things that weren't to be messed with.

'Ah well, that's what you get when you tie yourself into tradition.' An amused voice drifted across from the adjacent check-in line, a faint west-country burr lacing it, and he turned to look at the girl checking in next to him – obviously another snow-lover, was he completely surrounded? His intended cutting response never made it out of his mouth.

Ella carried on filling in the check-in documentation without looking up.

'Get hooked on traditions and you just set yourself up for a ton of stress when things don't work out,' she carried on. 'Can't see the point myself. Go with the flow and make the best of the situation, enjoy London in the snow for once. No one's died, although my will to live is on its last legs listening to you lamenting about some eggnog get-together. I'm sure your family will all still be there in a few days.'

Unlike her own, who'd never actually managed to be present often enough to qualify any situation as 'tradition'. To her the snow was an exciting twist to what would otherwise be a fun weekend away. Christmas shopping in London had been elevated to something a bit more magical.

She finished signing her name and glanced across to look at him, knowing she was probably about to get a mouthful but really not caring because he was sucking the joy out of the room. She looked straight into the eyes of the one person she'd never expected Christmas to throw at her again.

***

His mind slipped back down the years to the last time he'd looked into those almond-shaped hazel eyes with the slight tilt at the outer corner. Her hair was still the same light brown, not windswept by the sea air today but curling against her neck beneath a knitted beret. The fine-boned face gave her a fragile look that belied the girl he remembered. She had known exactly what she wanted and she took it without hesitation. His blood was pumping faster just at that recollection. Her nose and cheeks were pink from warmth

3

of the lobby after the icy cold outside and her eyes sparkled with the cheeky grin that now faded from softly curving lips. Her eyes widened as she looked him in the face and he knew instantly that she'd recognised him too.

'Ella Scott,' he said, her name returning easily to his lips without the slightest need for searching his mind. Wherever he'd buried that brief encounter - it must have been five years ago almost to the day - it clearly wasn't half as deep as he'd thought it was.

A brief pause as she clearly debated whether to acknowledge him or possibly deny she even knew him. Maybe even make a sharp exit. After all, that was what she'd done back then.

'Devon. Christmas 2008,' she said. The hazel eyes now wore a guarded expression. As well they might. She'd left without saying goodbye, leaving him to sleep on alone in his hotel room on the misty-cold seafront that last freezing morning before he flew out to Barbados, the Christmas family get-together not to be missed even back then. He'd never seen her again.

'What the hell happened to you?' he said.

****

He took his key card from the receptionist on autopilot, not even glancing her way, and took a step towards Ella, a light disbelieving frown touching his eyebrows as he looked her up and down. She pressed her teeth together hard and arranged her face into what she hoped was a neutral expression that would hide the fact that her brain was flashing a series of progressively more vivid recollections through her mind. Recollections that made her heart pound in her chest and her cheeks feel like they were on fire.

Oh my fuck he's seen me NAKED! Oh my life did I really DO all those things? With a STRANGER?

The whole point of a one-night stand was that you didn't have to worry about your behaviour being cringeworthy or about shocking your partner with uninhibited suggestions. Who gave a toss about a little thing like embarrassment when you were never going to see the other person again? You were in it for the moment, no consequences to think about. All you needed to do was make sure there were no repercussions that could come back and bite you on the arse in the future. She'd learned that from her parents, both of whom had failed epically on the no-consequences front, and there was no way she was going to repeat their mistakes. She'd made a clean break of it and walked away, no phone numbers, no addresses, no comeback.

Until now.

***

'You remember me then,' he said.

How could she not remember? One scorching night in her memory with nothing to taint it because she'd made sure she walked away immediately, before any of that could happen. She hadn't hung around to listen to him backtrack and talk his way out of the situation. She knew better than anyone what one-night-stands turned into in the cold light of day, and there would be no awkward morning-after goodbyes in the cold for her as he exited her life as quickly as he'd entered it. She'd circumvented that completely.

'I should have known it was you just from the complaining,' she said, not looking him in the eye in the hope that he wouldn't notice her blushing. 'I've never met anyone else before or since who goes to eggnog parties. Still heading out to Barbados every year then?'

She saw his eyes narrow at that and another memory came from nowhere, filling in one of lots of fuzzy blanks that fitted around the not-so-fuzzy images of hot sex. He'd been negative about the Barbados Christmas back then too, while she'd been fighting down a spike of jealousy. Not about Barbados, although of course if someone ever happened to offer her a ticket there she would rip their arm off in her eagerness for a luxurious beach break. More about a Christmas filled with your entire family. Christmas 2008 had been particularly sparse for her on that front, though she was used to it now.

'It's a family tradition,' he said. 'The whole point is that you repeat it on a regular basis.'

Family had come first with Tom Henley, she remembered that too. And clearly it still did. One-night stands were meant to only be about sex, but there had been hours of talking too, lying awake with the soft background sound of the tide and the slant of moonlight in the velvet darkness of the seafront hotel room. Maybe that was why he hadn't been relegated to totally forgettable in her mind. Sex was one thing, but they'd had more of a connection than just that. And maybe that was part of the reason she'd left, because she'd had a glimpse of what it could be like between them if there had ever been more than one night and it had been crystal clear at the time that one night was all it would be. No suggestion of more had made it to being verbalised by either of them.

When it came to leaving, all she'd really done was get in first.

He moved closer, not quite into her personal space but close enough to make her pulse jump. The intense expression on his face, as if he was remembering how she looked without her clothes, the way his eyes were fixed upon hers, the knowing smile touching the corner of his mouth, told her that hers wasn't the only mind being treated to a hot rerun of their last encounter. The burn in her cheeks refused to stand down. She needed to get out of here, away from that boiling hot gaze that was making her stomach feel like it was melting.

'So what are you doing in London?' he said, an interested smile crinkling the gorgeous grey eyes. 'How have you been?'

Oh my life it was *beyond* awkward. Her toes curled at his attempted polite small talk when surely his mind must be full of x-rated images from what happened last time they were in the same room. She glanced around her for an easy escape route and shifted her bag from one arm to the other, keeping her door key card in her hand as walked toward the curving staircase. He kept pace with her while she groped for a brush-off comment that would allow her to make a fast exit up the stairs.

'It's a long story,' she said, in a closed tone of voice that she hoped would tell him she wasn't remotely interested in relating it but he simply stood his ground and looked at her expectantly.

It was clearly going to take more than a hint to fob him off. She turned to face him.

'I'd love to catch up but I'm meeting someone,' she said.

***

A stabbing sensation deep in his chest felt like jealousy, but was clearly his pride kicking back in at her detached brush-off. Brief acknowledgement – check. Polite 'hello,' – box ticked. Tom Henley knew perfectly well that his next move should have been to continue with his stay at the hotel and let her do the same, keeping out of her way for the duration of his (hopefully short) visit. Separate ways well and truly intact.

That would have been the sensible next move, and the one suited to his life and to the way he thought he had categorised her in his head: fun evening, hot night, nice memory, no bearing whatsoever on the present.

Except that deep down he knew he was kidding himself.

Instead, the file in his mind that related to Ella Scott was *unfinished business* and it was her fault for simply disappearing. No contact, no saying goodbye. No woman had ever left him before or since and let's face it, it wasn't as if there'd been a shortage of opportunity. The demands of medical training combined with his regimented upbringing – boarding school, heavy on routine, heavier on expectations – had meant that the short-term relationship was the only type he had any interest in.

He knew absolutely zilch about her beyond her name and a bit

7

of background. And the fact that there was a silky inch or two of skin just at her inner hip that was so soft against his lips it had driven him crazy. He tightened his grip around the smooth leather handle of his holdall at that particular thought.

After she'd left, he'd been plagued with doubt that their unbelievable night really hadn't been all that great for her and this blow to his pride had bothered him for far longer than it should have done. Why should he *care*, as long as he'd had a great time? It wasn't as if she was the first, or the last. And he'd intended on walking away himself just a few hours later, just not in the abrupt cut-all-ties way that she had done. He'd become so accustomed to being the one in control, the one who backed away, that her no-show had been a bolt from the blue. It simply hadn't entered his radar for a second that she could walk away first.

Devon had been a stopgap for both of them. He'd been visiting a friend for a few days before his annual departure for the house in Barbados. She'd been on the Christmas break from her college course, working crazy hours in a restaurant on the seafront, making the most of the holiday overtime. Passing through, the both of them.

Instead of just leaving the encounter in the past where it belonged, it had remained a loose end in his mind. In the months that followed, his ears pricked up whenever he encountered a patient with the surname Scott, wondering randomly if it might be a relative of hers. Hankering after something he couldn't have and didn't need were diversions he couldn't afford and he'd made an effort to push the what-if from his mind ever since. Tom Henley didn't allow himself to be diverted from his path in life, not by anyone or anything. He hadn't been raised that way.

Now he had a few days staring at four walls while he waited for the airport to reopen. No friends to visit; they were all doing their own usual Christmas thing. And when he eventually got to Barbados it would be the beginning of a new era as he stepped into his father's shoes, the culmination of nearly thirty years of career preparation, and one which filled him with a crushing sense of being hemmed in.

With that prospect bearing down on him, the resurrection of a non-thinking, mind-blowing repeat of the most exciting, sensual encounter of his life felt suddenly like the Christmas gift to end all Christmas gifts. A brief respite before the walls closed in on his life in the New Year. Not to mention the fact that it would redress the balance and kill off that what-if once and for all.

She glanced at her watch and gave him a polite must-dash smile. Unfortunately, she wasn't looking like it was that attractive a prospect from where she was standing.

'Someone?' he clarified.

She stole a glance at the revolving doors as they spat another snow-covered guest into the lobby.

'A friend. She's actually due any minute,' she gabbled.

She? So not here as part of a couple then? His interest intensified at the revelation and he shrugged easily.

'She's probably delayed because of the snow. It's bad out there,' he said, stating the obvious. 'Can I buy you a coffee while you wait?'

An awkward pause and then she gave him a perfunctory smile.

'I don't think it would be a good idea,' she said, not really meeting his eyes.

'I'm getting seriously mixed messages here,' he said. 'There I was thinking you were instigating a rerun and you won't even do coffee?'

'A rerun?' she said.

'I suppose you're going to tell me it's a coincidence that of all the places in the lobby, you chose to stop and chat to me right here?'

She stared at him through narrowed eyes, wondering what the hell he was going on about, then followed his gaze as he looked up, one eyebrow cocked knowingly. An enormous bunch of mistletoe tied with a red silk bow was suspended directly above them. Her stomach made a warm, melting flip and she hefted her holdall in front of her as if to ward him off.

'Coincidence,' she said, her cheeks warming. 'Pure coincidence. I had no idea that was there.'

'Oh really?' His tone was amused, as if he didn't believe a word of her excuse and was thoroughly enjoying this, toying with her. And let's face facts, he probably was. Of course after her wanton behaviour of five years ago, Tom Henley thought she was an easy lay. And could she really blame him? Because five years ago for one night only, she'd been exactly that.

'No! I really am NOT that kind of girl,' she gabbled desperately, then saw his cocked eyebrow, his half smile, realised he was teasing.

She rolled her eyes at the ceiling and grinned as she looked back at him.

'I just realised how that sounds,' she said. She sighed and put her bag down for a moment on the marble floor, passing a hand over her eyes. 'Believe it or not I don't do one-night-stands, I don't actually do *any* kind of stand. What happened in Devon was a blip.'

'A blip?'

A smile played on his lips, as if having her on the back foot amused him all the more.

'A one-off,' she clarified madly.

It was true, that night in Devon *had* been a one-off, never repeated before or since. For some reason that night the conditions had been perfect for one-night-stand requirements. Need to prove herself alive – *check*. Don't-care attitude – *check*. Both had come from the loss of her grandmother a few months earlier, which in light of the fact that when it came to parenting skills, her mother and father had proved themselves on a par with a chocolate teapot, had meant Ella was truly on her own in life at the age of twenty-two. Add in the fact she was sacked from her waitressing job and that Tom had come to her aid, and mix in the fact that he was leaving the country the next morning. No repercussions to worry about when the other person was on another continent – right?

Result – a one-night stand that had been so hot it made her toes curl just thinking about it. And the whole point of one-night stands was they stopped at one night. The clue was in the name.

'It's nice to see you, Tom,' she said. She kept her tone detached, polite. 'But I really need to get settled in.'

This time he didn't follow her, but she felt his eyes on her as she took the stairs to the galleried landing above.

'Coffee,' he called after her. 'Open invitation, grab it while you can. The moment the snow melts I'll be out of here.'

CHAPTER TWO

She had absolutely no intention of grabbing it while she could.

It was perfectly simple. This was the UK after all, not Lapland. How long could the snow possibly last before he would be winging his way to Barbados as planned? One day? Surely two at most. All she needed to do was keep her head down and stay out of his way until Liz got here, avoiding any further encounters. Unfortunately, her ready-made excuse of a travel companion still hadn't shown up. A harried phone call later and she understood the reason why.

Turned out Tom Henley had a point. Liz's train was delayed by at least three hours due to snow on the bloody tracks. Plans to simply hang out in the room for a bit until her friend showed up suddenly morphed into the most boring waste of time imaginable.

Half an hour later and she'd drunk two coffees and eaten all the complimentary biscuits in the room. She bounced on the bed and glanced through the hotel information brochure for the second time, thinking it over. She could stare at four walls while she waited for Liz or she could while away some time in the award-winning Spa.

No contest. She stood up and tugged her swimsuit from her case.

***

A gorgeously relaxing ambience, muted lighting, fluffy towels and complimentary robes. The Spa was virtually empty, it being that lull just around lunchtime, between check-in and check-out. With all the snowy London sights to take in swimming wasn't a big daytime attraction. Ella swam a few laps of the pool, then climbed out and settled herself on a wicker lounger, magazine at the ready. Soothing background music filled the air. Bliss. Not a sign of Tom Henley anywhere. And of course there wasn't. With a flight on standby at any moment, Tom Henley was hardly likely to change into swimwear and be parted from his mobile phone, right?

Wrong.

Ten minutes later and she glanced up from her magazine to see him stroll casually into the pool, a towel slung around his neck, dark blue swim shorts topped with perfect tight abs, broad muscular shoulders and damply tousled dark hair. It seemed that for all his grouching about missing eggnog parties, Tom Henley was in no rush whatsoever to get back to the airport. Her heartbeat immediately picked up as if she'd done a couple of circuits in the beautifully equipped gym. She saw him clock her from the opposite side of the pool and he sauntered over leisurely.

'What, no friend?' he said, when he was a few feet away as if he thought she was some billy-no-mates with a fictional travelling companion. He sat down next to her, although the room was full of empty loungers and her stomach knotted into a ball of tension.

'Liz is delayed in the snow,' she said. 'A bit like you.'

She saw his eyes sharpen.

'So you're at a loose end, then? Time to kill.'

The look on his face was open and friendly. His smile was as melting as she remembered, the way it started slowly and then moved upwards to crinkle the corners of his eyes. And she'd forgotten he had a way of holding her gaze with his that made her limbs feel like they might turn to jelly. She forced herself to sound detached.

'Not for long. Just until her train makes it through, then it'll be on with the Christmas shopping weekend.'

'I thought you didn't do Christmas,' he said.

He was referring to the fact that back in Devon she'd turned the festive season into nothing more than a work opportunity, waiting table or bartending all the hours she could muster, all geared towards glossing over the fact that there was actually anything to celebrate. She was surprised he remembered that kind of detail about her and had assumed his recollections would be all about the bedroom.

'I don't.' She shrugged. 'Liz won a competition. A weekend for two Christmas shopping in London. She asked me along.' She glanced around the beautifully-finished opulence of the Spa. 'It seemed a shame to turn her down for a principle. Shame she's running late.'

He settled himself back on the wicker lounger next to hers, propped up on one elbow to face her, clearly intent on a proper conversation. And what the hell, maybe if she got it over with, did the whole small talk catch-up chat, he would leave her be.

'So how've you been?' he asked. She thought she saw genuine interest in his eyes now. 'You had another waitressing job lined up didn't you? Back in Devon. Did you finish college?'

A smile rose on her lips as she remembered her former self. Big dreams. Not on his scale of course with his medical training and his father's footsteps, but big for her who'd dropped out of school and drifted from one temp job to the next.

'I did,' she said. 'I did the jewellery course. I'm surprised you remember.'

A brief hesitation and then she held her small hand out towards him, a swirl of beaten silver on her forefinger. Without thinking he took it in his; the resulting flip in his chest at the touch of her soft skin took his breath away. When had he last been this on edge with a woman? His love life had been a bit of an afterthought these last months as his family piled on the work pressure. Without realising what he was doing he automatically checked beside the silver ring for a wedding band. There was none. She withdrew her hand and he let it go.

'I sell some of it online now,' she said. 'I've been trying to build up a business but it takes time. I do craft fairs, that kind of thing. And in between I still give good waitress.' She smiled. 'What about you?'

He shrugged.

'After you left Christmas went pretty much as planned. Then I went back and got on with my medical training.'

Again, pretty much as planned. *As planned* played a big part in his life.

She smiled. Her light brown hair was pinned up on her head and she wore a blue and white striped bikini which was far from skimpy but which still did nothing to hide her slender frame and long legs. Just looking at her like that made heat begin to course through him.

'We're from different worlds, you and me,' she said. 'You had your rugby playing, your future medical career, your public school background, your family, your life plans. I waited tables at a hotel in Ilfracombe that Christmas and I was sofa surfing my way around my friends. It's amazing we ever hooked up at all really.'

He remembered that. How she'd had no real base, no family ties, and most of all how she made that seem liberating instead of lonely.

She looked away, and he followed her gaze back across the glassy surface of the swimming pool.

'For a while I stayed with my Gran at this time of year but now I just go wherever the mood takes me,' she said. 'Last year I waitressed in a hotel in the Lakes – the Christmas lights were just the prettiest thing ever, but it was freezing cold. Even more than this. The year before that I did charity work in a soup kitchen and the year before THAT I was working my way round France.'

She counted off the Christmases on her fingers. He only needed one finger for his last four Christmases. Every single one had been the same.

'And this year?'

'I'm doing this weekend with my friend Liz. She entered some competition on the back of a breakfast cereal packet. It's supposedly for Christmas shopping, all expenses paid and some spending money thrown in. But I'm going to try and drag her round the sights a bit. Shopping's not really my thing.'

'What about after this weekend?'

'Well then I'm working again. I've got a waitressing gig back in Cornwall. In Looe. I lived there for a while with my Gran. Brilliant time for earning, Christmas, if you've got nowhere else you need to be. My speciality is unsociable hours. When this weekend is over I'm booked up right through Christmas and New Year, I'll barely have a minute to think. Whereas you'll probably be having cocktails at sundown and a leisurely break – right?' She sat back in her lounger and looked at him with interest. 'Come on then, give me a rundown of your last four Christmases.'

'Well I don't need to use my fingers to count them off, if that's what you mean,' he said. 'Touch down in Barbados a few days before Christmas. Catch up with friends and family. Head back after New Year.'

His tone was throwaway, unenthusiastic. Then again, mustering up excitement when you'd done the same thing year on year since you were a kid couldn't be easy.

'Your life is one big déjà vu,' she said, and seeing the fed-up expression on his face she couldn't resist adding, 'And where's the fun in that?'

There was a spark in his eyes as he held her gaze a moment too long and smiled, and she realised, too late, that he'd considered that comment a flirt. She whipped her eyes back down to her magazine, feeling warmth rise in her cheeks. She really ought to get her mouth under control and get this encounter over with right now.

'I'd better get back,' she said. 'Check my phone, see when Liz is getting here.'

She tossed the magazine onto a low wicker table and climbed off the lounger, being careful to swing her legs off onto the floor first to avoid giving an impression of beached whale. And since she really didn't have the confidence or the heeled wedges to pull off flouncing out in a bikini, she settled for wrapping the towel around her hips sarong style. She could feel his eyes on her as she walked away from him and then, just as she thought she was home-free, in her fluster she managed to take the left turn toward the crystal steam room instead of the right turn into the ladies' changing room.

The option was there, of course, to scuttle back the other way, thereby losing the unruffled poise she was doing her best to channel. But he'd shown no sign of following her so instead she opened the glass door and sat down on the tiled bench in the small square room, letting the hot mist wash over her skin. She could while away five minutes in here and then nip off to the showers with her poise intact.

She had the steam room to herself and she sat back with a sigh on the bench and leaned her head against the smooth tile of the wall. Closing her eyes, she breathed in the soothing scent of the aromatherapy oils clinging to the steam.

And then the glass door slid open and closed, letting the steam clear a little, and she was looking through the mist right at him.

Oh hell.

***

He ignored the empty bench opposite and instead sat down next to her. Up close the steam was clearer, she could see tiny droplets of water clinging to his hair.

'I thought you were heading out?'

Heat was pulsing through her that wasn't entirely down to the steam room.

'Changed my mind,' she said airily. 'Thought I'd have a quick steam first.'

As if she were a carrot or a stem of broccoli.

A pause that was long enough for her to wonder if he might actually just want to sit in silence next to her and take in the relaxing facilities, and then his deep voice echoed slightly in the tiled room.

'You ever think about it, what it was like back then?'

From time to time, when she couldn't sleep, but she wasn't about to tell him *that*.

Her heartbeat had leapt into instant thundering mode. Instead of answering, mad laughter cackled forth at the utter craziness of the situation.

'Ahahahaha! *It*?' she questioned preposterously. He didn't so much as flinch.

'*Us*,' he clarified. 'You ever think about us?' He lifted a hand and tucked a damp stray curl of hair behind her ear. 'I do.'

Her pulse was going crazy at his light touch and part of her, the part she really needed to crush into submission here, wanted to go with the flow. What the hell, let him go ahead, just to see if his kisses were as bone-melting as she remembered. She made a last-ditch effort to hang on to sense.

Rules, Ella, think about your life rules. They're there for a REASON!

'Tom,' she said, speaking slowly in the hope that it would make her voice steady and that he might actually listen to what she was saying. His thumb continued to stroke her jaw lightly. Her stomach was pooling with heat that had nothing to do with the steam. 'You're here for – what – a couple of nights while you wait for your plane to be rescheduled? If what you're hoping for is some kind of rerun, it's just not going to happen. I'm not that kind of girl,' she said. 'I never really was.'

'Where would be the harm?' he said. 'What would be the big deal? It's not like we haven't been here before.'

And of course he had a point. Any reservations had been discarded five years ago. They'd been intimate on such an intense level that maybe it was really no leap at all to pick up where they'd left off all that time ago.

She drew in a breath, ready to list all the reasons why, actually, it *was* a big deal. How it would be a regression, how it couldn't possibly end well, and then he stopped all planned protestations with a kiss. His hand slid back from her jaw to cradle the nape of her neck, his tongue slipped softly against hers and her stomach dissolved like melting toffee.

His hand slipped to her bare thigh, began stroking its way higher. Her mind followed it, inch by slow inch, although her eyes were tightly shut. He reached the delicate skin of her inner thighs and then his fingertips teased their way beneath the edge of her bikini bottoms. She gasped into his mouth as he slid two fingers inside her in one smooth movement and she felt him smile.

'Tell me again, why this is a bad idea,' he whispered, the ball of his thumb now beginning to circle her most sensitive spot, while his fingers continuing their slow rhythmic grind in and out. The sweet friction made her feel weak. Reasons jumbled into a mess of words in her mind.

'I don't do second-time-rounds,' she managed. 'Of anything. It's kind of like a personal rule of mine.'

'Still living in the moment then?' he said, holding her gaze. 'You haven't changed.' He smiled, moved his lips to her ear. 'No one around but us,' he whispered. 'I could have you right now and no one would see.'

The recklessness of it all had its own seductiveness, it took her straight back to the last time they were together. At the time, her own situation had been what drove her, the need to escape from the yawning absence of family and love that Christmas had been throwing at her from every angle. He had been the perfect distraction, a reason to disengage from everything that was going on around her.

No such excuse this time. In fact, all sense of rationality warned her off. Yet still there was the voice in her mind breaking through, reasoning with her, working with that physical desire for him. Where, really was the risk? He'd be gone in a couple of days, maybe even sooner. She would return to her life again just as she had before, unscathed. Couldn't she just step back into that moment again, enjoy a rerun of the delicious past encounter?

She let her own hand slide over his hot, damp skin, over hard muscle. He caught her fingers in his free hand as she reached his shorts. Her hand was drawn away and held still while he continued to stroke her, adding a third finger, increasing his pace, stretching and teasing until she could think of nothing else but the sensation. The steam room was forgotten, hotel was forgotten, self-preserving life rules were forgotten and she cried out against his neck as he took her over that delicious edge.

As consciousness began to slip back she realised shadows were moving outside the glass door, the heat was intense now and they were both dripping sweat. He withdrew his hand, not rushing, just as the door clicked open and a middle-aged couple took the bench opposite, vague outlines in the steamy air. She kept her head down as if they might by some super power know what they'd just been doing in here, stood up and tugged him by the hand out of the steam room and immediately turned left into the circular aromatherapy shower. He curled his arms around her waist, pulling her hot skin against his and she forced herself to STOP THIS RIGHT NOW. Her body might have been conquered by the heady combination of hot steam and his intoxicatingly expert touch but her mind still just about had a handle on reality.

'What now then?' he said, his voice was thick and she could feel his rigid erection hard against her. 'We could go up to my suite.'

The way they had five years ago? She'd been there, done that and moved on.

'I don't think so,' she said, disentangling herself.

'Really?'

'It's just not a good idea.'

He looked down at her, grin creasing the corners of his grey eyes.

'You're actually going to leave me hanging like this?' He glanced downwards.

She gave him a sweet smile.

'Of course I'm not, let me just fix that for you.'

She pressed the button labelled COLD and pushed him into the shower well.

CHAPTER THREE

He caught up with her by the exit, as she walked through the spa bar, cheeks still pink as she attempted to pull off a swift exit.

'Dinner?' he said, clearly not remotely put off by the cold shower.

She carried on walking, heading back through to the lobby while her heart made a mad sprint. Even without their history, he was asking her to dinner, and there was that niggling little question of when she'd last been asked out. Two years was it now? Liz would know, she was always trying to pressgang her into dates she didn't want. But her heart could sprint as much as it pleased, there were rules to be adhered to here, rules that she lived by for very good reasons and Tom Henley was a clear-cut case.

For speed, she figuratively threw Liz at him as an excuse instead of giving him the full on broken down reason that dinner was a non-starter, not least because her list of life rules seemed to bring out the exasperation in those of her friends that knew about them.

'It's been lovely to see you,' she breezed, 'but my friend should be arriving any time now and I really need to get properly settled in the room. And then of course we'll be busy, shopping, sight-seeing, you know how it is.'

Her mobile burst into life in her jeans pocket and she fumbled it out. Perfect timing. The screen informed her it was Liz. Obviously she must have arrived at Paddington and was checking in with a progress report. She flashed Tom Henley a confident see-how-busy-I-am roll of her eyes, and picked up. The line was awful. She came to a standstill on the thick pile carpet and moved to one side of the corridor to let other guests pass. Tom Henley didn't excuse himself, simply leaned against the wall and watched her with an amused expression in his slate grey eyes.

'You sound like you're shut in a fridge,' Ella said.

'That isn't so far from the truth.'

She had to focus hard to hear Liz's voice over the background crackle.

'You're *where*?'

Surprise made Ella forget herself and exclaim without thinking and she clocked, a second too late, his eyebrows raising almost imperceptibly.

There went her perfect excuse.

Liz's voice was faint.

'I'm in a train carriage somewhere between Newark and some other station at the ends of the bloody earth, waiting for someone to rescue me. And the buffet car's just run out of coffee.'

'How long are you likely to be?'

She turned her body away toward the wall and tried to talk into the phone without moving her lips while Tom made no attempt whatsoever to avert his eyes or look busy. Instead he was watching her, a small smile touching the corners of his mouth. For Pete's sake, where were his manners? He couldn't have eavesdropped more openly if he'd grabbed her mobile and pressed speakerphone.

'It isn't looking good.' Liz's voice was apologetic.

Conscious of his eyes on her, she took a few paces away from him, out of earshot and lowering her voice just to be sure, although why she was bothering she had no idea. It was perfectly clear that her big fob-off was trapped in the snow somewhere up North.

'You can't give up,' she pleaded through gritted teeth. 'I *need* you here. I've bumped into some guy from my past, we had a...' she searched for the right word. Just exactly what *had* they had?

'…fling,' she said eventually. 'A few years ago. He's asked me out to dinner.'

She couldn't bring herself to mention their more recent steamy (literally) encounter in the spa. It had been a lapse of judgement, nothing more. He'd caught her off-guard.

'And that's bad because?'

'Because I don't do the past. You know I don't.'

That attitude had afforded her a lot of face-saving and bravado in the past. It was tried and tested.

'That's just some stupid principle, Ella. It doesn't mean you're incapable of it.'

She might have known Liz wouldn't see it her way. Her friend was forever trying to fit her up with blind dates.

'You would say that though, wouldn't you?' she countered. 'You and Alfie are on-again off-again so often I can't keep track.'

'That's how the rest of us do it, Ella,' Liz said patiently. 'It's called give and take. That's how you get to know someone.' A pause, then, 'what's he like?'

Ella glanced back down the corridor at him. Tom smiled at her and nodded and her stomach gave another of those small melty flips. She tightened her grip on the phone.

'Too good-looking for his own good and won't take no for an answer,' she said out of the corner of her mouth. 'What are the chances of you getting here tonight?'

Liz's laughter was just audible over the crackly line.

'Tonight? Try the whole weekend. Have you seen the forecast? Imagine a snowball in hell and then lengthen the odds. By a mile. I'm getting back home before we resort to eating the weak.'

'For Pete's sake, Liz!'

'It'll do you good,' her so-called friend said. 'When did you last have a date? And look at it this way, if it's as bloody freezing there as it is here, at least you'll have someone to share body warmth with to survive.'

A couple of days stuck in the snow in London had suddenly taken a very nice turn for the better.

'Have dinner with me tonight,' he said again, as soon as she pocketed the phone.

'I can't.'

'Why not? Your better offer is stuck in the snow somewhere for the rest of the weekend.'

'That was a private conversation.'

He shrugged and grinned.

'Yeah well, it was kind of hard to miss. Come on, you're on your own now, I'm offering to buy you dinner. What exactly is it that you're afraid of?'

'I'm not afraid!' she snapped.

'Then what?'

She looked down at her fingers.

He watched as she took a deep breath before the knockback, not that he had any intention of taking no for an answer, no matter how many times or how many different ways she said it.

'I don't do the same situation twice,' she said.

'Living in the moment.' he said, holding her hazel gaze. 'Of course. I get that.' That had been something else so enthralling about her all that time ago. Unlike him, with his mapped out future and responsibilities, she'd had no agenda, no grand life plan other than to squeeze every drop out of every single experience she had. The memory of what that had meant in bed made heat begin to simmer in his veins. 'But still we didn't part on bad terms back then. Where would be the harm in us having dinner?'

Gentle fob-off clearly wasn't working so she cut to the chase.

'I just have rules about that kind of thing,' she blurted. 'Life rules.'

He was staring at her as if he thought she might be insane.

'Life rules,' he repeated.

She emphasised each point by counting them off on her fingers.

'I never go over old ground. I don't do the same situation twice. The past is the past. I leave it there and I only ever look forward – which are actually all the same rule said in different ways but that's how important they are to me'

She held his gaze boldly for a moment, giving him a chance to process.

'What kind of nutty way to live your life is that?' he said at last.

'You can mock if you like but it's actually stood me in good stead.' She shrugged. 'It's nothing personal. We had a great time but it was over with five Christmases ago.'

She held her hand up, five fingers extended, to press the point even further.

'You're knocking me back because of some crazy *life rules*? Is this some recent thing? How come you never mentioned them when we last met?'

'I didn't need to mention them then. It was the first time around.'

She saw exasperation fight with determination on his face. Apparently determination won because he came right back with a different approach. She had to hand it to him, he didn't give in easily. Most men she came across who showed an interest were easy to discourage with a firm no. Not that she was particularly snowed under in that department, her last date having been a brief affair months ago.

'You do realise you're working against higher elements here,' he said.

'What?'

She looked at him through narrowed eyes.

'Fate,' he said. He was watching her intently. 'Think about it. Everything about this encounter is down to luck. How many probabilities do you think we've bucked here?' He began to count off on his fingers. 'You're here because of a competition win, must be thousands of entrants, and now your mate can't make it through and you're here alone. Pure chance. And me? White Christmas in the UK. When did we last have one of those?'

She couldn't stop a smile at his refusal to give in. Obviously taking it as a sign of weakening, he leaned in towards her. She caught the clean woody scent of his shower damp hair. 'We were meant to meet again and do you *really* want to be the one to slap fate in the chops?'

'Fate, in my experience has a crap sense of humour,' she said. 'Best not to engage with it at all. I control my life, not the other way around.'

'I'm asking you to have dinner with me not jump into bed with me,' he countered.

She could feel her heart quicken, because wasn't there a part of her that wanted dinner? Wanted *more* than dinner? That brief hot encounter in the steam room still held her body in its grip. In terms of physical want and need, wasn't there something about him now that felt...*unfinished*?

Her mind, not completely turned to mush by his stomach-softening lopsided smile, and by what he could do with his hands, took the opportunity to remind her that however lightly she might portray it now, walking away back then had been no picnic. It had been a bit of a wrench in fact. By the end of that night she had been smitten and there had been a part of her that wanted to swap addresses, make future plans, see how it went. But her resolution had never truly faltered because she didn't need a crystal ball to know how things would turn out if she did.

Tom Henley was from a different world. Back then and still now. It could never have lasted. Why taint the perfect night by trying to prolong it? Long-term happiness could not be built on a chance encounter. OK so they might have made a strong connection, but it was still just a one-night stand. And she knew better than anyone that you couldn't build a future on one of those. Not the kind of future that fostered happiness at least.

Why resurrect all this now? It had been neatly filed away in her past and Ella Scott didn't do the past. She did the future, she did optimism, she turned a fresh new page every day and made her own happiness because she couldn't rely on anyone else to do it for her.

'It isn't about dinner or about sex,' she said. 'It's about principles. Something that's great the first time around shouldn't be revisited. You shouldn't mess with perfection, it will only be a let down in the long run. Nothing's ever better the second time around.' She gave him a breezy smile as she walked away. 'I hope your plane is rescheduled quickly and you have a good journey.'

'You're wrong,' he called after her.

She turned back and looked him straight in the eye. He was staring at her as if he thought she might be crazy, so she took a couple of paces closer so he could see she was serious.

'Classic movie remakes,' she said. 'The first time you visit Paris. Horrible cover versions of great songs. First kisses. Amazing meals. A new book.' She paused and added, 'Relationships.' She stood for a moment looking at him. 'It was a perfect night, a fantastic memory. How the hell could I possibly improve on it? Why would I *want* to?' She gave him a parting smile. 'I'm sorry. It was nice to meet you again but I never should have let it get beyond a quick hello.'

***

So he was a *fantastic memory*? His pride took a well-needed boost from that comment because for a while there as she gave him the brush off despite the way she'd melted into him in the spa, he'd been wondering if he was losing his touch. He'd wondered exactly the same thing five years ago in the weeks following that cold morning after a mind-blowing night when he'd woken up to an empty bed.

Finding out that the abrupt end of their time together had been down to *her* own reasons alone, completely insane though they were, was threaded through with relief that it hadn't been down to something lacking in him or his performance. And if it had been a *perfect night* and a *fantastic memory* he was surely in with a chance of talking her into a second round.

A winning smile for someone called Lucy at the reception desk was enough to get her room number.

CHAPTER FOUR

She had choice of the twin beds now that Liz wasn't turning up and most of her unpacking still to do. Disappointment rose a little at that; she'd been looking forward to seeing her friend. But still, if anyone was used to making the best of a situation, it was Ella. She'd made a lifetime out of it. She took the bed by the window.

Tom Henley stayed on her mind. As if it hadn't taken her long enough to stop him doing that first time around.

She'd hardly made a dent in the unpacking when the knock came at the door and her first excited thought was that by some miracle Liz had made it through the snow after all.

She rushed to open it.

'Good wine,' he said, leaning against the doorframe. 'That second trip to Paris where you take in all the off-the-track sights you missed the first time around. Favourite restaurants. Songs you hear for the first time on the radio and just have to track down. Tiramisu always tastes better on the second day. Boxing day turkey with pickles easily rivals the full-on Christmas roast.' His molten steel eyes took on a wicked glint. 'And sex.'

She stared at him.

'Are you going to invite me in?'

She stood aside, shaking her head lightly as if to clear it. He strode into the room and turned to face her. A hot flash of what had gone on between them last time they'd been in the same room as a bed made her cheeks burn and she folded her arms automatically as if to do so might ward the memory off. The last thing she needed was to think about how it had felt to be intimate with him, that road was paved with squashed resolve.

'What the hell are you talking about?' she said.

'Your principle is flawed,' he said, with a hint of triumph as if he'd invented the wheel. 'Just because something is fabulous the first time around doesn't mean it can't improve or be fabulous again. All those things I listed improve with time. Even better or at least as good the second time around.' He paused, holding her gaze mesmerizingly with his own. '*We* could be that.'

'How do you know?'

'How do you know we wouldn't be?' he countered. 'All rules have exceptions. Or loopholes.'

He was utterly gorgeous. And her stomach was melting.

'And the loophole in this case is…?' She somehow managed to keep her voice neutral.

'That what happened between us five years ago was cut short. By you, to be specific. It was unfinished. It didn't end for some bad reason. Therefore, technically, it isn't over. It's just been in limbo these past five years. It actually counts as one encounter.'

There was a delicious hint of flattery about his determination to persuade her which was *so* seductive. Being pursued relentlessly wasn't a sensation she'd experienced much. Her past was more about people running off out of her life rather than clamouring to stay in it, even for a short time. She kept her guard in place yet she couldn't stop the smile creeping onto her lips. He really was *impossible*. And funny.

'OK, you're really pushing the argument to its limit now,' she said. 'The last time I saw you before today I was in your bed. Are you actually suggesting we just pick up where we left off?'

She tried not to think about the steam room, because it under-mined her argument with herself and with him. She couldn't believe she'd let it get that far.

It had been a long time since she'd come across a guy who needed more than a firm 'no' to discourage him, mainly because she didn't let things progress far enough to need more than that to get out of it.

He spread his hands.

'There's no need to get so literal. I'm not suggesting you jump straight back into bed with me.'

The way he paused after that sentence made her stomach turn softly over, clearly because she hadn't eaten since this morning and absolutely NOT with disappointment. Because she most certainly did NOT want to jump straight into bed with Tom Henley.

'I'm here until the snow melts. Or the fog lifts. Or whatever bloody weather it is that's got the airport on lockdown. You're on your own because your mate hasn't made it through the snow. We're both at a loose end and how the hell does having dinner with an old friend contradict your bonkers life rule?'

The way he said that made her suddenly feel like she was over-reacting here, that she was reading far more into this than there was. It occurred to her suddenly that her heel-digging refusal might smack of caring a bit too much. Which she absolutely didn't.

Her mind spiralled back down the years to the icy walk to the station that she'd made herself take, knowing he was back in the comfortable but tiny hotel room sleeping alone. It might have only been one night, but she'd connected with him on a level she rarely did with anyone. It had taken strength to make herself get on that train, knowing she would never see him again. But she had done it. And she was convinced it had been the right thing to do. It had been about self-preservation. The past ten years or so, since she'd given up relying on her mother for any support, had been about building her own life and making sure there was no one in it that could knock her down. Did she really think she wasn't strong and self-assured enough now to have a simple dinner with the hot guy from her past without turning into a simpering wreck?

And of course there was a part of her that was curious. What had he been doing since they last met? He'd had his big life plan all mapped out, she remembered that much, and back then he'd seemed so excited about it. She didn't pick up that same spark of enthusiasm now and it intrigued her. What exactly had changed? He would be winging his way to Barbados again, maybe even as soon as tomorrow morning. The forecast was supposed to be improving. And she would finish her weekend in London and then go back to her life, exactly as she had done five years ago. A life that was a lot more successful now than it had been back then.

Where would be the harm?

Tom Henley meant nothing to her. What better way to prove it, to herself as well as to him, than to go out with him.

'Just dinner,' she clarified, narrowing her eyes.

He held his hands up, the picture of innocence.

'Whatever you like.'

***

Ella pawed through the contents of her luggage and realised she had absolutely no idea what Tom Henley's idea of a dinner date would entail. Mainly because the last dinner date they'd had involved eating fish and chips out of the paper while sitting on a harbour wall and looking at the Christmas lights draped around the marina. She let her mind drift back to the sting of the cold air on her cheeks, the sharp taste of the salt and vinegar, the scent of the sea.

Fish and chips had been a last resort because they'd been thrown out of the restaurant where she was working and he was eating. And that was the point right there. He'd been eating a late lunch with a group of friends at the most expensive restaurant in the town. He was flying out to Barbados within days. He came from a family of doctors who drank eggnog at parties. She looked at the selection of clothes she'd brought with her for the weekend with Liz and nothing jumped out that would make her fit easily into those situations without standing out.

Fish and chips out of the paper she could do. She gathered up jeans, vest and thick jumper. She'd just have to get in first and pitch dinner at her own level.

***

'I've booked a table in the restaurant,' he said, looking her up and down when she opened the door to his knock. He took in her jeans and UGG boots. 'It's got two Michelin stars, fantastic food. We can start with a drink in the bar if you like.'

'Actually I was thinking we could go out and take in a bit of London in the snow,' she said, grabbing an enormous parka from where it hung over the back of a chair and winding a scarf around her neck. 'Hyde Park's just round the corner with the Winter Wonderland!' Her eyes lit up as she slammed the door of her hotel room behind her.

'What about dinner?'

He followed her down the hall.

She flashed him a smile over her shoulder.

'That's not a problem is it? We can pick something up while we're out.' She took a few paces further and then turned back when he didn't follow her. 'Unless you'd *rather* go to the restaurant, in which case I totally understand.' She made it sound as if the restaurant served up slops instead of some of the finest dining in the country. 'You go ahead. I'm sure we'll bump into each other again for a quick goodbye before you fly out.'

Five minutes later, Tom was following her out through the revolving doors into air so clear and cold it felt like breathing in cut glass. Grit scraped beneath his boots on the pavement where it had been scattered to disperse any ice and the snow had stopped for now, leaving crispy clear conditions and the possibility that his journey might be back on track in the very near future. For some reason the delay no longer irked him as much.

34

Their breath puffed out ahead of them in soft clouds and it turned out inclement weather had its advantages. The buzz of people at Hyde Park Winter Wonderland was still there, but it wasn't overcrowded. Unfortunately it also meant the ice rink hadn't sold out. He attempted to dig his heels into the frosty path as she dragged him eagerly towards it.

'We could get a drink?' he suggested.

'We can do that afterwards.'

She turned back to him, the tip of her nose pink from the cold, her eyes sparkling and frost clinging to her hair in the silver glow of the fairy lights strewn overhead and all around them, and he felt his resolve falter.

In the centre of the rink was a Victorian bandstand and live music drifted across the ice. Parts of the UK might be at a standstill due to the blanket of snow but there was no sign here in the city of the fog that was blighting the airports. They seemed to have escaped the worst of it and there were plenty of people out enjoying the novelty of the bizarre weather.

'I don't do ice skating,' he protested. 'I haven't done since I was about six.'

'So what exactly is that you *do* do?' she asked, totally ignoring him and leading the way to pick out skates. 'Michelin-starred restaurants and family parties? What are you, fifty? What about the fun stuff?'

'That IS the fun stuff.'

'What size are you?'

She held his gaze belligerently until he grudgingly said 'Twelve.'

Five laborious minutes later and he was laced into a pair of plastic skates. For Pete's sake, it felt as if his ankles were in a vice. He struggled after her toward the rink, doing his best to stay upright. She sailed past him and did a neat little turn, then slowed down so he could keep up. Small children and couples holding hands bombed past them on both sides. The twinkly Christmas-ness of it added a surreal unreality to the situation. A couple of hours in her company and anything seemed possible.

And in a flash of déjà vu he understood. Hadn't that been the thing that was most intoxicating of all about her?

***

'You need to relax your knees a bit,' she said as he clumped awkwardly along next to her, upright and straight backed, as if he were on the conveyor belt walk at Heathrow with a suitcase and a manbag hanging off him. 'It's easy really, just all about balance.' The fact he'd given it a go despite his reluctance pleased her. The flash of a grin in spite of himself as he picked up speed gave her a glimpse of the guy she'd met back on the coast. The one who'd paddled in the freezing cold sea that late afternoon before Christmas, lifting her in his arms and threatening to dunk her in while she'd squealed with laughter. Afterward, they'd found a pub with a roaring log fire and he'd ordered them both coffee with a side of brandy to warm them up.

She moved smoothly ahead of him, keeping her balance easily. She hadn't skated for ages, but there'd been a rink in Bristol where she'd lived with her mother and gone to school. She'd done it often enough in the past to pick up the knack again pretty quickly. She was rather enjoying the superiority of it all, staying just in front of Tom so he could get the full benefit of her prowess, when a small child with an orange bobble hat and a manic grin careered into her at an insane speed. In a millisecond, self-assurance gave way to chaotic pinwheeling of arms and grimacing of teeth and then, with an unladylike squawk, she lost her balance and ended up part of a massive tangle of arms and legs on the ice. The kid disentangled himself, totally unscathed, and skated away while she looked up at Tom. A thin spray of ice coated her face and she could feel a cold damp patch soaking into the seat of her jeans and a sharp stinging on her left knee.

'It's all about balance, right?' he said, looking remarkably steady

36

on his skates and holding a hand out to her.

***

She grabbed his hand and was back on her now rather wobbly feet in one strong pull, leaning over to check her stinging knee and noticing that he kept hold of her hand. There was a tear in her jeans through which a bleeding graze was visible.

'Are you hurt?'

The concern in his voice brought a flutter somewhere deep in her chest. It was probably because the only person who ever had a stake in her well-being was herself. She stood up straight immediately and gave him a breezy smile.

'I'm fine. Come on, let's get going again.'

He tugged hard enough to stop her intended big flourish of a skate off and she saw him watching her with a steady calm.

'Let's take a breather and check out that leg.'

He pulled her by the hand to the side of the rink, somehow managing not to fall flat on his own arse in the process.

'I'm perfectly alright,' she protested all the way. He totally ignored her. For Pete's sake, she'd gone down hard. She was lucky she hadn't broken her bloody neck. He pulled her across the rubber skate matting to a quiet spot and made her sit down while he unlaced her skates and tugged them off.

'You've cut your leg. So stop with the moaning and let me check you haven't done anything worse.'

He held her foot, encased in its thick woolly sock, in his hands, and slowly rotated her ankle. Her eyes were drawn to the gentle way he cradled her heel, his thumb sliding slowly up her instep.

'Hurt anywhere?'

She shook her head.

'Only my pride.'

He ran practised hands up and over her knee, checking for swelling, and the unexpected slide of his hand over her inner thigh took her mind right off the sting of her grazed knee. He was kneeling in front of her, and he raised his head to meet her eyes steadily with his own dark grey ones, both hands moving over her leg with a touch that could now only be described as a stroke. Her stomach gave a delicious flutter that spread slowly lower to tingle between her legs and simultaneously rushed up to her brain to exhibit itself as clanging alarm bells.

She stood up sharply.

'I don't need looking after,' she said, adding a couple of paces to her personal space. 'I didn't need it five years ago and I don't need it now.'

He stood up next to her, feeling the distance she'd put between them, knowing it wasn't just a matter of physical space. His heart sped in his chest as if he'd skated a few circuits of the rink at full pelt instead of limping around it on two left feet. He'd forgotten how long and slender her limbs were, how her fine-boned fragility hid the fiercely self-reliant person underneath. A surge of protectiveness flooded through him, and the fact she didn't want his protection made her all the more alluring. She was her own person, now as then, not about to rely on him to take her through her path in life, determined to take responsibility for her own destiny rather than expecting him to make it happen for her. She felt like a clean crisp breath of icy fresh air, and it made his senses spin.

The elapse of time had convinced him she hadn't been all that – maybe *they* hadn't been all that. Self-preservation had made him tell himself he'd done the right thing in not looking for her when she'd run out on him. It had been the only way to silence the nagging thought that it was a mistake, letting her go like that without a fight. Not that he would have had much of a headstart on tracking her down, she'd made sure of that.

He'd known her name, but really, how many Ella Scotts were there in the world? And was she really Ella, or was it some shortened version of loads of other possible names? He and Ella had lived so deeply in the moment for that night that he hadn't even picked up on how little she'd volunteered about her family and background. He'd kicked himself after she'd gone for that, so self-absorbed had he been in talking about himself. Their conversations had been about hopes and dreams, future plans. They'd truly lived in a bubble of perfection.

He'd left her in the past, believed that it was for the best. And now a couple of hours in her company and he wasn't so sure.

***

He caught up with her as she went to return her skates. She pulled her boots back on, being careful not to use him to lean on for balance. Physical contact with him seemed to scramble her brain, and that spelled danger.

'You didn't need looking after back in Devon either,' he said. 'Remember when we met? That guy claiming you'd short-changed him with his bill.'

A smile rose on her lips at the memory.

She remembered the flickering tea lights on the tables in the restaurant. The too-big Christmas tree in the corner that had snagged her clothes every time she walked past it with plates balanced on her hands. She'd worked in smarter restaurants in her time, but the pay had been good, a friend of hers had got her the job for the busy festive season and she was grateful for the distraction. Her first Christmas without her Gran. Celebrating didn't even make it onto her to-do list. It hadn't really done that since either. Christmas was a money making opportunity to her, and that was the way she kept it.

'He was drunk as a skunk and chancing his luck,' she said. 'But you stepped right in,' she grinned as she remembered. 'You were still squaring up to him, even as I got the sack and we were both thrown off the premises!'

He laughed and she smiled back. He'd been the most stunning guy in the room, sharing a table with a group of mates, a cut above

39

the local clientele with his relaxed designer clothes and dark good looks. The other waitresses had clamoured to serve his table. Not Ella. She needed money, not complications. And yet when he'd stepped in like that he'd elevated himself above the usual dross. Because she wasn't used to having family or friends stick up for her, let alone total strangers.

'You did pour a pitcher of beer over his head,' he pointed out. 'I don't think I can take the full credit.'

How cold and fresh the salt air had been after the heat of the restaurant and kitchen as the door had slammed shut behind them and she'd found herself alone and looking up at him on the icy pavement. The first person to wade into a battle for her since her Gran had gone. That was where it had started for her, they'd been together for the next fifteen hours, but with the benefit of hindsight she knew now that her heart had been vulnerable to him from the moment he stepped in. Awareness was a great thing. She knew her weaknesses now when it came to him, and getting in too deep this time around just wasn't going to happen.

'Exactly my point,' she said. 'I didn't need your help.'

She could enjoy his company, spend a few days with him, but at the end of it she knew she'd be able to walk away.

CHAPTER FIVE

He handed her a cup of mulled cider and she blew on its steaming surface, breathing in the delicious scent of sharp apple and sweet cinnamon. They found a bench and he sat down next to her and she looked out across the rink, the white fairy lights giving it a magical touch. Music from the band drifted across the ice.

'There you go,' she said. 'Isn't this loads better than sit-up-straight napkin-in-your-lap fine dining? You can keep your Michelin stars.'

Her eyes sparkled and the tip of her nose was pink. He wanted to kiss it.

'OK,' he conceded. 'Maybe it was. Maybe I've got a bit stuck in a rut of dinner in restaurants.'

'Is that what you've been up to then, since we last met? Fine dining and behaving responsibly?'

The dullness of his life smacked him squarely between the eyes in the face of her vibrancy. He took a sip of his cider, the alcoholic kick of heat spreading in his abdomen.

'You want a potted history? I can give you that in the space of about a minute.'

He could hear an edge of bitterness in his own voice and he curbed it, forced a neutral tone. Wasn't that what he'd been doing for years now? Forcing himself to be neutral, not to feel aggrieved or resentful. He was duty-bound after all. Resentment of that was a pointless waste of time.

'After we met I finished my medical degree. Then I did a couple of years foundation training as a junior doctor.' He paused. 'Then training for general practice.'

'With your father?' she said.

He nodded. His had been a family strong on tradition, generations of doctors before him.

'That's right.'

'He must be really proud of you, following in his footsteps like that.'

There was a wistful edge to her tone that registered somewhere in his subconscious. He didn't answer that. He wasn't really sure pride came into it. He'd known his long-term career plans for so long that sometimes it felt like he'd been born with them. Any prospect of deviating from them might have been possible once, but not anymore. Not since his father's stroke and the slow decline of his health.

'So you'll be a GP in your home town. At your family practice?'

'That's right.'

'You don't sound so thrilled about that,' she said. 'I thought you wanted to work abroad. Weren't you going to work as a medic in war-zones or poor areas or something?' She shrugged. 'Maybe I got that mixed up, it was a long time ago.'

A wistful pang stabbed him somewhere below the ribs and he jumped a little as it made him realise how resigned he was to letting go of that particular dream.

'That was just an idea I had back in college,' he said dismissively. 'It never came to anything. Things change. My priorities didn't allow for it in the end.'

And so he'd gone on to GP training instead of specialising elsewhere.

'Your priorities?'

He shrugged.

'Family stuff,' he said vaguely. 'Would you like another drink?'

'What about girlfriends? she said, when he sat back down, her voice completely neutral as if she couldn't care less. It gave him a surge of hope that she asked at all.

'No one special,' he said.

At first that had been down to the hard work and gruelling hours of his medical training. Later, when one relationship after another failed in its early stages, he had to admit that maybe there might be more to it than that. Accused of being distant, of not really investing himself fully in the relationship, in actuality his lack of interest hadn't been conscious. Unfortunately the kind of woman who really spiked his interest was the kind who had little inclination to settle down to a by-rote predictable life. Unfortunate, because with his life mapped out the way it was, that kind of woman would surely be the perfect addition to the jigsaw.

Had there been anyone since Ella, with her drive to have fun and live in the moment, who'd really rocked him? For the first time he wondered if his lack of interest when it came to women could have anything to do with that short encounter with her in the past. She represented perfectly all the things he denied himself – freedom, unpredictability, no ties to hold her back, no guilt. Her life was well and truly her own.

'What happened to you?' he said suddenly. 'Why did you just leave without saying goodbye back then?'

She shrugged.

'I just thought it was fitting. Why prolong it? It was no big deal really, was it? You were off to catch your damn flight out of the country. I had a train to catch.' She paused. 'Also, I hate goodbyes.'

'We could have kept in touch.'

Not that he had intended that at the time. It had only occurred to him afterward, when the decision had been taken out of his hands.

She laughed.

'And how exactly do you think that would have worked? Where exactly do you think we would have gone from there, Tom? You were off to your huge family in Barbados and then back to Oxford, big career all mapped out. Lifelong family commitments. Just where exactly were you thinking you could slot me into all that? I was going to wait tables over Christmas and borrow a friend's sofa for a while.'

He didn't answer. She had a point.

Ella cut her eyes away from his and looked down at her cup.

'I didn't really think I needed to say goodbye,' she said. 'We'd be going our separate ways the next morning anyway. I thought you'd be glad I made it so easy, I spared you that awkward who-uses-the-bathroom-first thing. And I look like Shrek first thing in the morning; trust me, I did us both a favour.'

A surge of surprise coursed through her that he was actually bothered. She hadn't imagined for a moment he would give her leaving a second's thought all that time ago, when she'd shrugged her way into her jacket and crept out of the hotel and into the dim light of the early morning, freezing rain stinging her cheeks, mist clinging to the sea. Except possibly to be thankful that she'd made it so easy for him.

They'd both known what it was. Each knew they didn't fit the other's life. She was hardly about to tell him that walking away without saying goodbye had been her safety net. It hadn't been the sex, unbelievable though it had been, it had been the talking, the way he'd stroked her hair and held her. That night back in 2008, Ella had felt special. She'd felt safe. And weren't those also the exact reasons she'd backed away, taking control of the situation at the last moment? They were also the reason that her stomach was now fluttering softly and her heart rate was set to speedy.

Ella watched him closely. He didn't disagree, he simply took a sip of his cider, and she could tell from his you've-got-me expression that she was spot on. His life had been mapped out back then and it was even more so now – he was just a few years further down his plotted path. Just the thought of it made her feel claustrophobic.

'Five years later and we're still polar opposites,' she said. 'Our lives are totally different. I did you a favour by leaving, it would only have turned into some goodbye love-in, and who needs that kind of schmaltz?'

Not that it had really been the fear of schmaltz that had put her off staying; a chance would have been a fine thing. It was more the thought of him backtracking, trying to undo the night they'd spent. She hadn't wanted it to end up as that, some inconsequential embarrassed morning after. It would have belittled it. It had been a funny, crazy, happy night and she'd wanted it to stay that way. Perfect in her mind.

But he had regrets. It was absolutely clear. The twist of excitement that this knowledge caused in her stomach was full of danger and she took a big swig of her mulled cider, hoping its warmth would spread there and take it away. She forced a breezy smile.

'Is that what this is really about?' she said. 'Closure? Did I deprive you of that by not staying put to say goodbye? Trust me, Tom, I did us both a big favour. It would have just been awkward. What do you think we would have said to each other before we disappeared back to our own lives? Thanks for a night of great sex?' She shrugged. 'I couldn't see the point.'

She couldn't face the rejection, more like. But she wasn't about to tell him that. Not after the years she spent since her teens, steeling her heart and telling herself there was no room for looking back in her life. She had bigger fish to fry in terms of regret, and not swapping addresses with Tom Henley came way down the list.

His smile melted away.

'That's all it was to you?'

She made herself hold his gaze.

'That's all it was, period.'

***

Well that put him straight and he really should be pleased. A true one-night stand with no complications was just the way he

45

liked it. And based on what she'd just said a repeat performance right now would have all the same qualities and the same lack of drawbacks. No bombarding with texts when he cut contact, no phone calls, no angst.

He ignored the twist deep in his stomach that felt a lot like disappointment. He had no room in his life for that. He stood up, held out his hands and when she took them he tugged her to her feet.

'Let's get something to eat,' he said.

The refined Michelin quality dining had, in her company, morphed into chips and hotdogs with a side of curry sauce as they walked between tiny log-cabin stalls selling everything from pretzels and sweets to gifts. He watched as she stopped near a jewellery stall, taking in the display of silver pendants, beads and bangles.

'I'd like to take a stall here,' she said, excitement lighting her face. 'I do quite a lot of craft fairs but this is something else. The fairground rides, the market stalls, the ice rinks, imagine the footfall you must get.'

'So are you still drifting up and down the south coast, job to job like you were before?' he said. 'I thought after you finished college you might settle down.'

She watched him suspiciously. Was this some attempt to angle for an address, some way of pinning her down? Good luck with that. She shook her head.

'I do travel quite a lot for craft fairs and markets,' she said. They began walking again. 'The odd thing is that I kind of thought I had put down roots. The few years before I met you I was living with my Gran. She had a cottage in Looe, in Cornwall. Tiny little two up two down thing, but it was lovely being there. I was having a nightmare at home with my mum and Gran stepped in and offered me her spare room for a bit.' A wistful smile rose on her lips. 'It turned into more than just a bit. I found work at some of the local hotels and restaurants and I started saving up to go to college.'

The familiar, dull ache when she thought of her grandmother and the cottage on the Cornish coast that had been home for a time, just after her mother finally moved in with one of her squeezes instead of moving on to the next one the way she usually did. A loathsome car salesman called Gordy who had wandering hands and who made Ella's skin crawl. No way was she living there. If that was what was going to pass for normal family life, she'd much preferred her mother's unplanned absences, thanks very much. The cottage had been the one place where, for those interim few years, she'd felt grounded and secure.

She'd felt able to commit to a college course with her Gran behind her and a sense of steadiness at last, a place to stay during the holidays. She'd long loved the sea, right from her sporadic visits as a small child and her love of the coast had never left her. She'd even begun to think she might stay there herself when her course finished, perhaps do some waitressing to support herself while she tried to get her dreamed-of jewellery business off the ground. Her Gran had been full of encouragement.

He was watching her, sharp interest on his face.

'What about when your course finished? Are you still based there now? How come you aren't still living with your Gran? I don't remember you mentioning her last time we met.'

She shook her head.

'I never mentioned a lot of things last time we met,' she said. She took a deep breath. 'She died nearly a year before I met you. She'd been ill for a while, it turned into pneumonia and she was just too weak to fight it off.'

How desperate Ella had been for her to fight. Yet still she'd slipped away. And security and love had slipped away with her. Ella had come to the conclusion that she wasn't meant to have that kind of life. She could count on herself and that would have to do.

'I'm really sorry,' he said, and when she glanced at him she could see he meant it. 'You should have said.'

She was long-practiced at glossing over the past. It wasn't even that hard anymore.

'It was a fling, Tom,' she said. 'I wasn't about to give you my life story when I knew we only had one night. We were living in the moment, remember? The whole point of it for me was to have fun, not work through my grief and family issues. Can you imagine if I'd started in on that – you'd have run a mile.'

'You don't know that,' he said, his tone indignant enough to make her look up. 'You make me sound like I was just after sex.'

She laughed out loud at that.

'Wake up and smell the mulled cider, you idiot,' she said. 'Wasn't that exactly what both of us was after?'

***

A slow walk back to the hotel, the cold really biting in the air now. She could see the moisture in the headlamp beams as they crossed the road and the grit crunched beneath her feet. The what-next hung in the air between them, so strong she could almost feel it. She'd made it crystal clear to him. She had life rules. The steam room encounter had been no more than a slip. And this would be no more than dinner. Yet still she wondered if he would make a move or if this would really be an end. A proper end to them this time.

He walked with her up the stairs and through the lobby, both of them having collected their key cards at reception on the way past. No going their separate ways in the lobby. Her pulse rate was going crazy as she walked up the curving staircase, the surroundings paling because of her heightened awareness of him next to her.

Her door came first.

She stopped outside, key card in her hand, and turned to smile at him, trying to make it an arms-length breezy friendly smile, not a come-in-and-jump-my-bones one.

'Thanks for a fun evening,' she said. 'It was good to see you again.'

48

'You too,' he said. She looked up at his easy smile, trying to imprint it on her brain so she could replace the previous memory with this older version of Tom. The same molten grey eyes but less of a starting-out-in-life sparkle in them. Instead, this version of Tom was broader, stronger and more serious.

He was close enough that one small movement would be enough for him to pull her against him or for her to step in and kiss his cheek perhaps. If either were to crack it would be him. She was sure of it. She was the one who'd left that morning by the sea, not him. She had the stronger will. Yet still he made no move. Anticipatory tension hung in the pause between them. It was so strong she could almost feel it crackle. Finally she could stand it no longer and turned to slide the key card into the lock.

'Enjoy the rest of your weekend,' he said from behind her.

She gave him a parting smile.

'Safe journey,' she said. 'Merry Christmas.'

The lock clicked and she opened the door. With every slow motion moment that passed she expected him to make his move, reach out, tug her back, and then…who knew how the night would end. And then the door was closed against her back and she was alone in the dark hotel room.

Alone except for her stupid pride, of course.

CHAPTER SIX

Tom stared at the polished wood of the door with its glossy scarlet number plate, and shoved away the hideous plummeting sensation deep in his abdomen. It was that same desperately sinking feeling he remembered from five years ago, but this time it had an added twist of triumph because he hadn't been the one left behind while she walked away. There had been a moment back there when to kiss her would have been so easy. The decision was within his control, his choice not to go any further. He'd wanted to redress the balance and now he'd done exactly that.

Dodged a bullet there, he was sure of it.

He walked down the passage and rejoined the stairs. Up to the top floor and his own suite where a fire had been lit and subtle lighting switched on around the room. The sitting room with its velvet sofas was the epitome of opulent luxury. But it could have been a broom cupboard for the amount he noticed it.

Triumph was a pretty hollow sensation, it turned out, when you'd won it by playing safe. He'd walked away because she walked away last time. Because his life now didn't allow for it. Because it could only ever be a couple of days.

None of those reasons seemed remotely significant now.

***

After the steam room she'd thought it was a forgone conclusion how the night would end, despite the way she'd knocked him back afterwards in the shower. Had he been waiting for her to make a move? Was that what this was about? He'd taken her at her word then, decided to respect her choice not to let this second encounter end up in bed.

Or after an evening in her company had he now decided she looked a whole lot better looking back? She'd forced him to go out with her instead of eating a civilised meal in the fabulous restaurant. Her plans, apart from waitressing here and there, barely scanned into the following week, while his pretty much took him the full way up to retirement. She still didn't fit in with his life and it was a hundred times more obvious now than it had been back then. She stared at her face in the bathroom mirror, cheeks pink, teeth gritted, barely able to stand still with unrequited tension. And finally, unsure what the hell she intended to say or do, knowing only that she would drive herself mad within the space of ten minutes if she didn't at least ask the question and find out what he thought of her, she crossed the room at speed and threw open the door.

He stood inches away from her, knuckles upraised in a mid-knock of thin air. She caught her breath.

'You see,' he said, holding her gaze steadily with his own. 'Fate.'

He moved at the instant she did, and then his arms were around her, his mouth crushed against hers, and she sank her fingers deliciously into his hair.

***

The kiss was a visceral moment for him, a burning uprising of suppressed desire for her, filled with five years of comparisons, five years of remembering her when the whole point of dating (which he'd done to some excess for a while there) had been to keep things forgettable. He realised now how laughable the idea of leaving her in the past really was. A part of him was still lying in that bed, looking in disbelief at that opposite empty pillow.

It was her. It always had been her. That maddening feeling of unfinished business when he'd been on the cusp of life.

He'd forgotten the way she curled her hands around his neck and that she liked to pull her fingers through his hair. His stomach simmered at the feel of it.

The way her body responded to his touch, his kiss, felt like slaking a thirst that she hadn't known existed. Yet maybe there was a part of her, deep in her subconscious, that had known all along the inherent danger in this moment. The part of her that had told her not to talk to him in the lobby, not to have coffee with him, not to have dinner, to try and backtrack after the steam room. She hadn't listened. Resolve was fuelled by self-preservation and it had diminished in strength with every moment she spent with him.

Too late, she recalled in all its full clarity her state of mind as she headed for the station five years ago. She had known she was walking away from him because she was too afraid to stay and accept the kick-in-the-teeth rejection that would surely come. She couldn't bear to hear it from him. And so she made the break herself.

Now it all came back in a flood of memories and delicious sensation.

Her heart hammered, reminding her how in-deep she really had been last time she saw him, and proving that she'd been kidding herself all these years; telling herself it hadn't been mindblowing, that it was just her memory playing tricks, in the way that in your childhood memories it always seemed to be sunny.

She'd been caught out by her memory playing tricks once too often. It had been easy to convince herself Tom Henley wasn't the dream she'd thought he was. She had her stupid ill-judgement of her father right there to prove that point. Memories couldn't be trusted. And going back was a bad idea.

Yet here he was, bucking that trend.

He backed her away from the door at urgent speed and she moved with him blindly, not thinking or caring whether furniture was in the way. His arms slid around her, grinding her against him as if he couldn't hold her closely enough. One of his hands tangled in her hair, tilting her head back to deepen his kiss and she could taste the faint twist of spiced apple on his tongue. She could feel the press of his erection against her, rock hard, and she ground her hips against him, secretly thrilled that she invoked that acute arousal in him.

Carefully laid safety nets pinged away in her mind. Guards slipped. She could think of nothing except that she was back in his arms.

Her fingers found the buttons of his shirt, the urge to feel his skin against hers so strong that nothing else mattered. She tugged them free, slid impatient hands up the taut warm skin of his chest. Her mind vaguely registered differences, similarities. The faint scent of his aftershave, still the same brand, something fresh that reminded her of the sea. A scent she associated with the salt air of the coast and a time when she'd felt truly happy. He felt broader now, his pecs rock hard, his arms roped thickly with muscle. He must work out.

His hands caught up a twist of her sloppy joe sweater and tugged it over her head. The instant it was gone his mouth groped for hers again, his hands moving to her jeans with unstinting urgency. She found his buttons, pulling at his clothes with an urgent kind of madness, and then the back of her knees hit the edge of the nearest twin bed and she was falling back. The soft velvet of the counterpane against her bare back, his bare skin against her own.

And it felt like she was meant only for him.

***

Naked now, clothes thrown aside randomly around the room, he cupped the firm swell of her breast in his hand, followed it with his mouth, closing his lips over the hard peak of her nipple and teasing gently with his tongue until she moaned and arched her back. He trailed his fingertips lower, tracing the smooth hollow between her breasts, lower still over her flat stomach and between her thighs to stroke softly at her swollen core. Delight surged in his stomach as he felt how wet she was. He slid two fingers inside her, a further spike of desire kicking in as she moaned her pleasure against his neck, then found the swollen nub at the very core of her and circled it slowly with the ball of his thumb, feeling her jump and writhe beneath him as he found a slow rhythm.

She clutched at his shoulders, her head thrown back against the counterpane, exposing the smooth cream of her slender neck for him to kiss. He moved back in surprise as she wriggled from beneath him, batting his shoulder aside, wondering if this was about second thoughts. She scrabbled through one of the open cases, toiletries and clothes flying as she tossed them aside and returned to him with a condom between her fingers. A surge of desire rushed through him at her smile and put paid to any further delay. Wanting to possess her fully, nothing else mattering, five long years of her memory driving him forward, he rubbed the swollen head of his erection against her slick entrance until she was writhing against him with desire, and when he could stand it no longer he thrust forward smoothly to the hilt. The moan of visceral desire escaped his lips before he could stop it.

Forcing himself to move slowly now, building up a delicious friction between them, he tangled his hands in the softness of her hair and took her with long and tantalising strokes until her breathing quickened and her legs curled around his back, her hands sliding down his back to try and push him deeper inside her. Responding to her every movement, he pushed them both towards that delicious pinnacle, taking his time, holding back to keep them hovering there as long as possible until her cries of pleasure pushed him over the edge and he could control it no longer.

Afterward, she lay panting, clutched in his arms, her own fingers digging into his shoulders in a tight grip, his breath deep and hard against her neck. Slowly, the firm stroke of his hand against her climbed down to a soft caress. Her mind began to filter in awareness of surroundings and background sounds.

A continuous high pitched eeee-aaaawww eeee-aaaawww cracked its way into her formerly preoccupied consciousness. It sounded like a donkey on acid.

'What the bloody hell is that noise?' Tom whispered softly into her hair.

***

She jerked her head up like a meerkat and gave the room a quick once-over. Tom sat up and rubbed a hand through his hair as she pulled herself off the bed, dragging the sheet along with her, giving him a glimpse of perfect creamy thigh and smoothly curved backside. His stomach began to heat up again just at the sight.

She picked her way across the shoe strewn floor to the corner, one hand holding the sheet against her chest, and righted the table he vaguely remembered knocking over. Next to it was the telephone and she replaced it on the table and put the receiver back. The high-pitched squawking stopped.

Noise removed, he glanced around the room. It looked as if there'd been some kind of explosion in a department store.

'Bloody hell, what happened in here?' he said.

He raised eyebrows at her and she tilted her chin up indignantly and folded her arms around the sheet.

'What do you mean, what happened? *We* happened.'

'We didn't do all *this*.'

He waved an arm around the room. Every available surface was littered with belongings, make-up, clothes. The opposite twin bed was covered in clothes and he shifted uncomfortably and pulled a trainer out from underneath him.

'I hadn't finished unpacking,' she said defensively.

'I thought you were staying here for the weekend, not moving in,' he said as she crossed the room back to him, picking up an armful of clothes as she went with her free hand.

She swatted him on the arm as she passed. The physical contact made him jump, his consciousness was so finely tuned to her every touch that it didn't seem to matter whether that touch was affectionate or not. Add in the fact that she wasn't wearing anything underneath that sheet and he wanted her again. More urgently by the second.

'I remember your hotel room back in Devon,' she said, dumping the clothes on the opposite bed and sitting down next to him, sheet swathed around her body, creamy shoulders exposed that were just made to be kissed. She blew a strand of hair out of her eyes. 'That one perfect suit-carrier and matching designer holdall. Everything in its place. I bet you even use the trouser press and laundry service, don't you?'

He grinned at her good-naturedly, leaning up on one elbow.

'That's what they're there for. Enables you to travel light.'

'Yeah well, I'm never sure what I'll fancy wearing until pretty much the moment I put it on,' she said airily. 'Makes sense to bring a broad selection.'

'And are you always this untidy?'

She glanced around the chaotic bedroom.

'This is *not* that untidy,' she said. 'You're obviously not used to sharing a room with a woman.'

She had him there. He wasn't used to sharing. Either a room or his life. For a while after he'd last met her he'd had a run of short relationships. None of them had been serious, not that he had given them the chance to become that.

So the no-second-time rule was well and truly broken and she would just have to work with what she had. Part of her was so busy feeling like jelly from post-shag euphoria that it overshadowed the more sensible part of her that couldn't believe what she'd gone and done, giving in to impulse over sense. Well, done it she had, and the only option she had now was damage limitation. Communicate a don't-care attitude and make it clear this wasn't going to lead any further than it had five years earlier.

'Don't be getting any ideas,' she said, raising her eyebrows at his obvious inability to take his eyes off her. 'I might have let myself get sucked into your whole *'loophole'* argument. But hey, it's Christmas right? I figure I'm allowed a little fun. You could be gone as soon as tomorrow. This is never going to be more than a day or two. So…' she took a deep breath, stood up, looked down at his amused expression '…same as last time. No looking forward or back. This is only ever going to be a fling. No strings, no thinking outside the moment. We enjoy it while it lasts and when it's done, we go our separate ways.'

She smiled into his gorgeous grey eyes and invested everything she had in the guard she'd honed to perfection over the years. She wasn't about to lose her heart to him. Not when she'd just about managed to hang onto it the first time. She was even stronger this time around, she was prepared. She'd built herself a career, a future, that didn't rely on anyone else and which therefore couldn't be lost or messed with. She wouldn't be giving up any of that on a whim.

'Deal?' she prompted.

Tom leaned forward and grabbed her around the waist, sweeping her into an arc over his body until she was lying on her back on the messed-up bed, and he began to unravel the sheet from her body inch by delicious inch.

'Deal,' he said. What else would he say? What else could this ever be? In the New Year he'd be taking on further responsibility, another step in his life plan, no room for impetuousness or rash decisions – he had people relying on him. What the hell else could he do – tell his sick father to stuff it, that the medical practice would have to manage for the first time in fifty years without a Henley at the helm because he wanted to jet out to warzones and charity work?

Just like last time, all she wanted from this was a fling. And just like last time, that was all he had to give.

CHAPTER SEVEN

The vibration of his phone brought Tom round and he automatically reached out to grab it from its customary spot on the bedside table without even really waking up. One semi-conscious hand closed over it just as he leaned a smidge too far and then there was a disorientating jerk as he managed to stop himself falling out of bed at the last moment by slamming a hand and foot out onto the floor.

Why the fuck was the bed so tiny?

No sun streaming in through billowing muslin curtains across the glass door that led out to the verandah. Instead the room was shrouded in the semi-darkness of a dawn in winter, in London. It thudded into his sleep-fuzzed brain then in one big tumble and his eyes widened in shock.

Grounded flight at Gatwick. Bonkers British weather. Lavington Hotel.

Except when he stayed at the Lavington the room was always one of their best suites and the bed was always a king-size. He turned over as best he could on the foot-wide chunk of single bed that was available, and there she was. His stomach gave a crazy flip at the sight of her.

She'd been curled up against his back like a child, hogging at least two-thirds of the narrow bed. The sheet was bunched up around her waist, revealing the long slender legs that made his pulse race just by looking at them. The soft swell of her breasts was visible above a twist of sheet that she clutched to her chest and her light brown hair fell softly against her cheek. No wonder the bridge between sleeping and waking had seemed blurred. She really was the stuff of dreams.

Somewhere in the small hours they'd finally fallen asleep after screwing every ounce of energy out of each other. And for the first time in he couldn't remember how long, he felt alive. He reached out to stroke her cheek, just for some confirmation that she was actually real and not some figment of his imagination. Her skin was cool satin. She shifted slightly in her sleep and he moved off the bed as gently as he could so as not to wake her.

His mind shifted back to the previous night. Her crazy rules. *Live in the moment, no regrets.*

The impulsiveness of being with her was intoxicating, a soothing antidote to what had become his suffocating, stifling life. It felt like sweet freedom, and he wanted to savour every second of that, because he knew it couldn't last.

He moved away from the bed, and went into the tiny ensuite to check his phone. A voicemail message from his mother in Barbados ('*...when are you arriving, Darling? Everyone's been asking after you...*') The age-old sense of responsibility tugged at him. Under normal circumstances that message would have brought a surge of exasperation at the unexpected delay, anger even that he was letting everyone down.

He checked the weather app on the phone, all ready to see the tiny snow icon that had dominated the wretched thing the day before. He frowned. No sign of the blanket fog lifting but there was no more snow on the way for now, and that meant the airports would be back in action pretty soon, right?

The information should have had him jumping for joy. So why the hell was he closing the app down with a sinking sensation of disappointment coursing through him?

He moved back out of the bathroom and glanced across the room at her, shoving the disappointment aside. This was a fling. It couldn't be more. She didn't want it to be more, he couldn't *give* more. They'd made the situation clear the previous day. They barely knew each other beyond the physical, hardly enough to base even the most short-term future on.

He could cross the room right now, slide his hands under the sheet, pull her against him and pick up right where they'd left off. That would be all she expected, those were the parameters they'd agreed to.

Instead, he found himself picking his way quietly around the room, collecting up his clothes and trying not to trip over her insane mass of belongings. She didn't stir in the semi-darkness, and he didn't expect her to since it was still too early for winter light to brighten the room, but he let the door snick shut quietly just in case.

***

The cold silver of winter morning gave the room a muted light that woke her up slowly. The usual second of disorientation that always happens when you stay somewhere new for the first time kicked in. It wasn't something that had ever bothered Ella. Moving around so much for craft fairs and just her itchy-footed desire to keep moving before things went tits-up meant she was used to adapting quickly to new places. Travelling heavy helped of course. She sometimes wondered what it said about someone that everything in their life with sentimental attachment could be squashed into a couple of suitcases.

Tom slipped back into her mind on the back of that second when she found her bearings, just the way he had done every morning at first after she'd left five years ago. How long had thoughts of him persisted? Not long. She was good at bricking things up in her mind, was a past master at it in fact. Crushing of memories

61

combined with telling herself it hadn't been all that. A tried and tested self-preservation exercise.

He wasn't here.

The bedroom was a pigsty, clothes and half-unpacked belonging all over the place, where she'd never got around to putting them away since he'd come back to her room, after that interim goodbye that neither of them had been able to stick to. Not a single item belonging to him fell into her sightline.

She threw the sheet back and crossed to few paces to the small en suite. The shower unit was bone dry. It was as if he'd never been here at all, as if he'd disappeared.

Which, her fully-awake mind now insisted, was clearly the *point*.

Now she knew what yesterday had been about for him, why he'd pursued her so insistently until she agreed to first coffee, then dinner, then bed. After the delicious night they'd spent together it turned out that it had all been about *closure*. She'd walked out on him five years ago, leaving him hanging. For Pete's sake he'd even told her openly last night that she was the only person ever to do that to him. It had been all about taking back control, reclaiming the upper hand. And what a fool she'd been for thinking it could possibly have been about anything else. This was *her* life after all, he was only doing the inevitable. It seemed everyone she ever came across had an exit strategy from her life. There was something about her, something intangible that she'd never been able to identify, that put people off, that put their teeth on edge, like running fingernails down a blackboard. Unable to work out what it was, her only option had been to stop people mattering so it wouldn't hurt when they made the inevitable exit.

She'd got in first last time and the no-second-time rule would have meant she left it at that. But no, she had to meddle with it, didn't she?

The sick feeling of disappointment in the pit of her stomach was only matched by the anger she felt at herself for making the same mistake she'd made so many times before.

Back to Plan A, from which she should never have deviated.

Half an hour later and she was showered and dressed, ready to head out. The whole *point* of the weekend had been to Christmas shop, not that she had a shedload of people to buy for, but there were lots of Christmas markets to check out, full of crafts and gift stalls, and even if she didn't have a big shopping list, she could look for some inspiration for her own jewellery designs. Perhaps next year she might be able to take a stall here instead of doing the usual waitressing. In a few years time she might even be able to drop the backup waitressing work altogether. The only area of her life with any long-term plan was her work and she refocused her mind on it, hard.

The brief double-tap at the door came just as she was ready to leave and she opened it, assuming it would be housekeeping wanting to service the room. Not one tiny speck of her thought it could possibly be Tom. That's how resigned to this kind of thing she'd become. She'd learned not to hope because there never was hope.

The gorgeous lopsided smile on his face as he leaned casually against the jamb melted away when he took in the expression on her face and the fact she was wearing an outdoor coat.

'What are you doing?'

He stood up straight. She floundered for a grasp on the situation and went with her original plan. OK so he might not have disappeared under cover of darkness, but reality had still bitten. She should never have let things get this far. She'd been swept up in the magic of Christmas and fun excitement and she'd taken her eye off the ball. And that led to nothing but trouble, and down the line, hurt.

'What I came for,' she said, winding her scarf around her neck to make a point, although the temperature inside the room was tropical. 'I'm going shopping. Christmas lights on Oxford Street.

What's the point of coming here if I don't go and look at them?'

He stared at her with a bemused expression on his face.

'Did I miss something?' he said.

'Your flight, maybe?' she said, picking up her enormous tote bag from the luggage rack beside the door and hefting it over one shoulder.

There was a sudden movement behind him and she looked up to see him step aside to let a skinny hotel porter through the door, pushing an enormous silver trolley in front of him that was groaning under the weight of silver platters, plates and cutlery. He glanced between them, Tom still waiting to be invited in and herself in her coat and scarf.

'Room Service?' he said doubtfully.

She locked confused, questioning eyes with Tom's mellow gaze.

'Full English breakfast, selection of pastries, toast and preserves, coffee, tea, muesli and selection of fruit…' the porter's voice trailed off as neither of them acknowledged him '…for two?'

A pause, and then Tom said, 'I ordered a selection. I wasn't sure what you'd like.'

Her mind reeled and heat began to work its way slowly up her neck to burn in her cheeks.

'You ordered breakfast,' she said, as if saying it out loud might make it seem more believable. She could hear the surprise in her own voice. Far from hightailing it out of her life without so much as a word, he'd ordered half the dining room to be carted up to her bedroom.

'Showered, changed, ordered breakfast. I would have used your ensuite but there was…' he coughed '…a lot of your stuff in there. And I didn't want to wake you. I'm an early riser,' he added to the porter, who was staring at them as if they were both insane. He jumped a little and shifted from one foot to another while Tom dug out cash for a tip. Then he left the room as if it were on fire. Tom turned back to face her. Just the two of them now.

Tom turned back to her.

'Where did you think I was?'

She could see from the cynical look in his eyes that he was making the connection himself and knew it was far too late to talk her way out of the situation. She'd jumped to the wrong conclusion about him; one that didn't paint him in a very happy light.

She shrugged.

'On your way to Barbados,' she said. 'I assumed the airport must have reopened-'

'And that I'd just had what I wanted from you and left without a word. Treat you with zero respect. Get you back for Devon, right?'

Her cheeks felt hotter than ever. He was annoyed. And really, he had every right to be.

'You were the one that walked out back then,' he pointed out unnecessarily. 'I didn't leave you hanging then and I wouldn't now. I let you sleep in, I didn't see the need to disturb you when all my stuff was in my room. And the conclusion you jump to, without so much as checking, is that I'd run out on you. Well, I'm not that kind of person.'

And by implication of course, he clearly meant *she* was.

'Why didn't you call my room?' he went on. 'Or check in with Reception if you were worried?'

She hadn't done either of those things because she hadn't needed to, so certain was she that he'd gone. She had a lifetime of experience to back up her jump to that conclusion and to hear it as concrete news from the receptionist would have made it all seem far too real and wounding. Better to just gloss over the whole thing as if it never happened.

Clearly she was insecure to the point of irrationality.

Her brain now told her to carry on as she had been doing, to just leave him and his insane feed-an-army breakfast and head off shopping. He hadn't behaved as she'd expected and she didn't need this, didn't need the unpredictable *caring* of it.

Yet at the same time she felt absurdly, uncharacteristically touched by it. His thoughtfulness in not wanting to wake her, the over-the-top but no less sweet for it gesture of surprising her with half the breakfast menu.

Really, how was he meant to know he was dealing with a basket case here?

She crossed the room to the table, unwound her scarf, and sat down on the edge of one of the chairs. Plates of food, teapots and cutlery covered every inch of it. She glanced up as him as he joined her.

'I'm sorry,' she offered. 'I thought—'

'You thought I'd run out on you,' he said. 'I can't tell you if I'll still be in the country tomorrow. Fantastic as I am, I can't actually control the weather.' He reached across the table for her hand and her stomach began to flutter as his fingers closed over her own. He held her gaze in his. 'What I can promise you is that I won't drop off the planet without saying goodbye.'

She felt so childish now, like a kid running away to avoid getting in trouble, that the urge to offer some kind of explanation, however crap, was irresistible. That in itself rang alarm bells. Why, if she didn't care what he thought of her, should she feel any need to justify herself to him?

'I just have this thing,' she said. She took a slice of toast onto her plate, began to spread it with butter, so she wouldn't have to look him in the face. It felt somehow unreal to have gone against her instincts to bolt. 'About goodbyes. I hate them. I avoid them wherever possible.'

'I had noticed,' he said.

She gave him a wry smile that lifted his spirits. For a moment there he'd thought she was going to leave him to the heap of food and disappear. That she'd decided to stay and talk, felt like a victory. It was certainly further than he'd got with her last time around.

'With me it's the other way around,' he said. His appetite seemed to be non-existent, but he went through the motions anyway. The meal was the background he needed to keep her here, keep her talking. He uncovered one of the hot breakfasts and cut half-heartedly into a slice of bacon. 'However much I might want to run away sometimes, I can't.'

She looked at him, a light questioning frown creasing her forehead and he shook his head at her.

'Doesn't matter.'

She picked at her toast.

'I don't understand. What could you possibly want to run away from? You've got it easy. Your life is charmed.' She put her elbows either side of her plate and began to count off on her fingers. 'Successful doctor, supportive family you love you to bits, holiday home in Barbados, family home in the Cotswolds, no money worries…'

He held up a hand to stop her. With every new point she made the weight of it all bear down on him. And the worst of it was the guilt it invoked. She was right. He was selfish for wanting to follow his own dreams.

'You're absolutely right,' he said. And maybe it was the knowledge that this was just a blip, something that wouldn't exist beyond the next couple of days, that she was someone who didn't know his family and could never communicate to them his hideous selfish disappointment with his own life. 'But you don't understand how it is with my family. And my work.'

He finally gave up on the cooked breakfast and pushed the plate to one side. His appetite showed no sign of returning.

'For as long as I can remember I've wanted to be a doctor,' he said. 'I've always looked up to my father, and the medical practice was such an integral part of our lives that it would probably have been weird if I'd wanted to do anything else. There was never any question in it for me. My grandfather was a doctor too, same town. And his father before him. There's been a Henley as the doctor in our town for over eighty years.'

And if he had a quid for every time he'd been given that piece of information he could retire right now.

'Of course these days it's not just one village doctor doing the rounds. We have a proper medical centre that services some of the surrounding villages too. My father is senior partner.' He took a sip of his coffee. His mouth felt dry. 'For now at least.'

'What do you mean 'for now?'

'He isn't well,' he said. 'I thought there would be time for me to build my own experience as a medic. The idea of settling down as a village GP seemed so far off that it never bothered me, I knew that's what my family expected me to do eventually and I guess I saw it as something I'd do when I settled down with a family. In another ten or fifteen years maybe.'

'That's why you seemed fine with it the last time we met,' she said. 'You told me about the practice then, but I've got to be honest, you seemed a shedload more positive about it all then than you are now.'

He nodded, offered her a rueful smile.

'Last time we met I was just qualifying. I was so wrapped up in that I wasn't really thinking ahead. Since then I've done foundation training, had time working in A&E, as much on the frontline as you can be in this country. 'It confirmed my own ambitions.'

She was looking at him steadily.

'You wanted to work abroad,' she said.

He nodded.

'I want to make a difference. Work for a charity for a while, maybe in war-affected areas, or where there's been a national disaster. Somewhere I could really feel I was doing something to help.'

'And have you ever discussed it with your father?'

He pushed his food around on the plate. How many times had he come close to broaching that subject? He'd put it off so many times.

'I didn't see the need initially, I thought I'd get my training out of the way first, then have a talk to him about my longer term plans. But then he had a stroke last year and he just hasn't properly recovered. He went back to work, downsized his hours, but he wants to retire now and make the most of his health.' He shrugged. 'I can't blame him for that. And of course he believes it won't affect the practice because he has the next Henley waiting in line to step up to the plate and take over.'

'You?'

'Exactly. How can I tell him I'm not up for that now when I've spent nearly thirty years with that as my life plan? He's been through so much this past year, and my mother too, supporting him. He's so proud and happy that I'll be taking over. I don't want to upset him and set him back. I'm meant to be taking the helm in the New Year.'

'And you don't really feel like cracking out the champagne.'

He shook his head slowly.

'Being a doctor is what I wanted. Being a village GP is what's expected of me.'

He stood up from the table, tugged her up next to him. Then he pulled her into his arms and kissed her, burying his hand in her hair. She curled her arms around him, understanding that maybe this was what he wanted from her, needed from her. Distraction. And that was OK, she could do distraction, it had its own appeal for her, especially at Christmas time when everyone moved in family groups and had their own exciting plans. Wasn't distraction partly what flings were all about?

And then he was stepping away. She stared at him, confused, as he reached for her coat, discarded on the back of a chair.

'What are you doing?'

'I thought you were going shopping?' He helped her into it.

'I was.'

'Want company?'

She stared at him as he opened the door for her and then followed him down the passage to the stairs, her heavy boots sinking into the thick pile carpet, confusion rising in her mind. So it wasn't just about sex then? Unless he found sightseeing an on-par distraction.

'For someone who's here on a Christmas shopping weekend, you don't seem massively keen on shopping,' he remarked, as yet another department store's sparkly festive window display failed to entice her inside. Women and shopping were in his experience hard to keep apart and yet they'd stopped for coffee twice, not to mention lunch, and still she hadn't bought a thing.

She didn't really do London pace either, strolling along Oxford Street and letting hordes of shoppers pour around them.

She smiled.

'I feel a bit bad, spending all the shopping money when Liz is the one who won the prize,' she said. 'I think I'll post it to her. Not that I'm mad keen on shopping anyway.' She glanced sideways at a window display, hampers filled with champagne and chocolates and luxury food. 'Liz had a massive list of people to buy for. Nieces and nephews and cousins coming out of her ears. I don't really have all of that.'

Her voice was matter of fact.

'What about your parents?' he said. 'Won't you see them over the holiday?'

She laughed mirthlessly as she came to a brief standstill outside a jewellery shop.

'That's nice isn't it,' she said, pointing at the silver display in the window. She didn't meet his gaze, instead looking through the glass at the bangles and bracelets and rings. 'I don't see my father at all. Haven't done for years. And my mother will be on a package holiday somewhere hot. Tenerife maybe.' She glanced sideways at him and began walking again. 'We don't really speak.' She touched his arm briefly to make him look at her. 'You're lucky to have a family who care about what happens to you. But that still doesn't mean you should let them dictate your whole life for you. No one should deny their own hopes and dreams in favour of someone else's.'

He looked away, kept walking. She stayed alongside him.

'I don't expect you to understand. You're obviously not from a close-knit family, you're self-sufficient. You've followed your dreams in a way I could never think of doing.'

'Why not?'

He'd already said more than he meant to, he could hear the hard edge in his own voice.

'It's complicated, Ella. It's not just about me. I can't just put myself first and then sleep like a baby at night. I have people relying on me. It's about duty and loyalty.'

'Surely your first loyalty should always be to yourself.'

How could he explain to her, when her family had clearly let her down so epically, that his entire existence for as long as he could remember had been geared towards fulfilling his family's expectations?

'I'd like nothing better than to have a proper family but it still has to be about give and take, doesn't it?' she went on. 'Otherwise it's just one-sided isn't it?'

'There *has* been give and take,' he said. 'For as long as I can remember I wanted to be a doctor; that's never changed. My parents have always supported me in that, and that ambition has always delighted both of them. My father has always talked about the day when I would join the practice and carry on the family tradition.'

'And now you have.'

'Yes.'

'And it isn't all it was cracked up to be.'

He dug his hands into his pockets.

'I guess I just never thought further than qualifying at first – it's such a slog to reach that point. You invest so much in it. Sacrifice so much. When I met you last time my long-term dream was to work abroad, maybe join Medicins Sans Frontieres, go somewhere where I could do some real good. On the frontline if you like. At that point it seemed an achievable goal. But then, when I qualified, it became clear very quickly that the path my parents expected me to follow was very different. And I'm just not sure I can bring myself to disappoint my father by blowing all his dreams out of the water, not when his health is so shaky. And it's not like I haven't gone along happily with those dreams all these years.'

'There must be some middle ground you can find, some compromise,' she said.

If only he could see a way to achieve that without risking further stress to his parents.

***

Early evening darkness had fallen now and the day had slipped past easily in her company, even with shops thrown in. Unheard of for him. They reached Trafalgar Square and Ella stopped and stared up at the twenty foot fir tree covered in hundreds of white lights. Fountains were lit up and crowds of people lingered in the cold to listen to carol singers.

'This is gorgeous,' she sighed.

'Even for someone who doesn't do Christmas?'

'You can talk,' she said. 'You've lost touch with the English Christmas. Not that it probably isn't *lovely* to lie on a sandy beach somewhere and sip cocktails. But you're hardly invested in all the magic stuff, are you?'

'And you are?' he countered.

She grinned. He had a point.

'Maybe I am,' she said. 'A little bit. From the outside looking in, that is. I'm not going to be scoffing Christmas turkey and mince pies, and I don't even have a Christmas tree where I rent, but that doesn't mean hot sunshine and a bikini would ever float my boat. That's just wrong. Christmas is meant to be freezing cold and you're meant to live in UGG boots.'

As she watched the carol singers, he slipped arms around her from behind and breathed in the sweet scent of her hair, liking the way she leaned back against him.

'It's snowing,' she said, and he looked up.

It was. Tiny, fine flakes of snow fell in the glow from the tree lights. And what had invoked teeth-gritting anger and frustration yesterday morning as it thwarted his travel plans, had no such effect now. She turned in the circle of his arms to face him, her arms sliding around his waist, her face upturned to his, nose pink from the cold air. Specks of snow clung softly to her hair.

'Question is, is it the *wrong* sort of snow?' she said, pressing an emphatic finger to his chest.

He realised with a spark of uneasy surprise that he hoped it was *exactly* that. Let the whole of the UK be buried in *feet* of the stuff. He didn't care if his flight never made it off the ground and it had nothing to do with boredom at the much repeated family Christmas traditions.

He wanted to be with her.

'Let's hope so,' he said.

CHAPTER EIGHT

A day out around the London sights and now dinner for two in his suite. Like a proper couple. It was as if this was a mini-break and they had a real life somewhere to go back to. She let her mind follow that fantasy for a while as they shared a bottle of wine and talked. She had thought limiting this to a fling would somehow automatically pitch them at that level and make it entirely about sex. She hadn't expected talking and getting to know him. This time around she found herself liking him way beyond those parameters, and dangerous though she knew it was, she couldn't help finding signs in his own behaviour that he felt the same. The way he'd spoiled her by ordering half the restaurant for breakfast, the way he'd listened to her plans for her jewellery business as if they hadn't already been to bed and he still had to jump through those hoops.

And now he refilled their glasses and she stood up to follow him over to the velvet sofa and the crackling fire in the grate, anticipation knotting in her stomach at the thought of being intimate with him again.

And then his mobile rang. She watched as he checked the screen, literally saw the change in his face, and when she ran it through her mind later on she recognised it as the instant when the real world kicked back in.

He took the call, phone pressed to his ear, subconsciously or not, his shoulder was now tilted in her direction as he turned away and took a few paces away. She could pick up the gist of the call just from picking up the odd word from his side, she could hear him discussing departure times, transfers, social plans. It didn't take a genius to know what the call was about.

'My mother,' he said, when he'd hung up. His expression was thoughtful and his focus was not there in the room.

'Is everything OK?' she asked, although any fool could see it wasn't.

He shook his head lightly as if to clear it.

'She's just stressing because I've been delayed. My father's had a couple of bad days apparently.'

She gave him a questioning look.

'It's not been easy for her,' he said. 'He's needed a lot of extra support. Especially at first when he first had the stroke, but the rehab has been slow and he gets so frustrated at the time it takes to make progress.'

Sympathy twisted in her chest.

'It must be very tough. I can remember when my Gran was ill. It was awful.'

Tom's mind spiralled back eighteen months. He toyed with the phone absently, thinking that he should check in with reception for any messages, call the airline. She was watching him, leaning against the back of the velvet sofa, her glass of wine in her hand and giving him her full attention.

'It *was* a tough time. At first there was just this awful shock, and the worry that he might not pull through it. I had to be strong for my mother, she was beside herself. Then once we knew he was going to be OK there was this time where you hope things will get back to normal. I knew the reality of it of course because of my work, I knew it could take time, months of physio, that kind of thing. And he's done really well. He's been able to get back to work, on and off, reduced hours of course.'

'That must be a relief.'

He nodded.

'It is. But it did bring it home to me that he's not getting any younger. He looks his age now, which he never did before. And he gets tired very quickly.'

The constant undertone of worry for his parents, resurrected by the phone call, now gnawed at him. He felt guilty because he hadn't made it to Barbados, and this guilt which he'd managed to crush whilst he'd been in Ella's company, resurfaced at full strength. He hadn't even called the airport yet today to check, he'd had to fob his mother off with yesterday's weather report. His sense of responsibility kicked back in at full force. What was he playing at here, indulging himself in a no-strings fling when his family needed him?

'My mother wanted to know if there was any news on my flight.' He made a move towards the door. 'I need to call the airline and maybe reception will have an up to date weather report. I'll be right back.'

How easy it had been to just let himself exist in this bubble the past few days. All the time, reality had been waiting just outside, ready to yank him back into its realm. He had family responsibilities, people relying on him. If he was fast enough he could still make Barbados in time for Christmas.

As he left the room Ella felt a surge of stupid disappointment, anger at herself for feeling insignificant. She might be an attractive distraction for a short while but that phone call represented the real world for Tom. Something she wasn't a part of either back then or now.

Her heart flipped into hideous lurching freefall. And the worst of it was the humiliation because she was expecting this, had thought herself *prepared* for it. Of course he was going to be rebooking his flight the moment he was able to. For Pete's sake, she was supposed to be pulling off *realist* here. What the hell was the disappointment about? Had she actually thought for one second he might have considered delaying his departure somehow, that he might have really been thinking of a way to factor her into his future plans? This was about sex, nothing more, she'd made that clear herself from the outset, how could she blame him for acting accordingly now?

This situation was playing out in exactly the same way as it would have done the first time around if she hadn't cut it short back then. And she had no one to blame but herself for letting it happen. She should have stuck to her no-second-time rule.

Had it really felt like they were a proper couple in this room? The magic dissipated the second he disappeared and she gathered up her cardigan and closed the door on the luxury suite where she didn't belong. Had she really been fantasising that she might? She went back to her own twin room, picked up the stack of leaflets in the hotel information file and forced herself to focus on planning the following day's outing. Solo this time. Maybe a trip on the London Eye? Or she could go to Knightsbridge and drool without spending at the jewellery in Tiffany.

A swift double tap at the door and she crossed to open it. She took the leaflets with her in one hand, to let him see she was perfectly fine; she could do London tourist weekend perfectly well by herself, thank you very much.

'The airport's open,' he said the moment she opened the door, and her heart felt like it sank to the pit of her stomach.

She caught her breath, made an enormous effort to arrange her face into a fine-with-me posture and stood aside to let him into the room.

'What time's your flight?' she said. She tried hard to pull off couldn't-care-less in her tone of voice.

'Half past ten.'

They had an hour or so then realistically before he would have to get to the airport for check-in. She swallowed hard, forced herself to nod. There was no point trying to deny it to herself, it was way too late for that now. She was in too deep. The déjà vu feeling of disappointment and inevitability churned in her stomach. She recognised it from last time and knew that any conviction she'd walked easily away from him last time was just a delusion. The only person worth denying her feelings to now was him.

This was the end then. An end they both knew was coming, one that they'd been in agreement on right from the outset. She covered up her sadness by emphasising the practical and readied herself for his leaving in the only way she knew that worked. She began backing off.

'You'll be wanting to get packed then,' she said brightly. That was good. That sounded like she was absolutely *fine* with this. She forced her gaze away from his and automatically took a couple of paces back. *Distance*, that was what was needed now. Get some distance in there now, before he did.

'No, Ella, I won't be wanting to pack,' he said, his voice exasperated. 'Unlike you I don't take half a dozen bags with me just for a weekend. I'll throw a few things in a case in the morning and I'll be away.'

Her heart gave a sudden little half-skip.

'The morning?' she said.

He nodded.

'Half past ten. Tomorrow morning.'

She drew in a sharp breath. He held her gaze steadily in his own. One last night together.

He pulled her towards him, lacing his fingers through hers. He hadn't mentioned *them*, what would happen to them tomorrow, and why would he? They'd both known from the outset that this was a fling. Same rules as last time. And that meant tomorrow morning it would be over. Why should she expect him to mention it when she'd made her own point of view crystal clear from the very beginning? Yet she already felt the wrench deep in her stomach. She shoved it from her mind with all her might.

Live in the moment.

She'd repeated that mantra to herself so often over the years that you'd think it would have a bit of clout now when she really needed it.

***

It was not the mad crazy sex of the last couple of days, the hungry rush for each other. Not this time. Tom wanted to savour her, to try and imprint on his mind how it felt to be with her. No wild tearing off each other's clothes, no half-dressed fuck because they were both too charged up to do anything but rush.

This time he kissed her slowly, slid his hands beneath her shirt across smooth skin, making the most of every moment. She pulled his sweatshirt up and over his head, threw it carelessly to one side, and then her hand found the button of his jeans and tugged until it came free. He pushed them down and away. Her fingertips played lightly over his erection, teasing, driving him crazy.

He breathed in the scent of her hair and her light floral perfume, slid his lips across the smooth skin of her neck, and then she raised her hand to the centre of his chest and pushed him gently backward until he reached the nearest bed. He sat down and watched as she stepped out of her jeans and threw her panties aside, then climbed onto the bed and walked on her knees until she reached him, his back against the velvet headboard. He reached for her, curling his arms around her waist and pulling her gently into his lap, finding her mouth with his. Her small hands cradled his face as she kissed him. He could pick up the faint hint of white wine on her tongue. She wriggled softly against him until she could slide her legs each side of him. Hotly aware that she was wearing no panties beneath the shirt, he felt her smile against his lips, leaving him under no illusion that she knew exactly what she was doing to him, while she ground her hips lightly against his raging erection. The sensation was unbelievable, maddening.

He groped for the buttons of her shirt with his fingers, tugging the garment roughly open until he could ease the soft weight of her breasts into the deep open vee of it. He leaned forward and took the tight peak of a nipple into his mouth, sucking lightly, grazing the hard tip gently with his teeth until she sighed and arched her back. Sliding his free hand lower, he found her swollen entrance with his fingertips and a rush of satisfaction at how wet she was, how ready for him. He stroked delicately, teasing her with his fingers until she squirmed against his hand.

Before he could lose all control, he curled his arms around her, turned her gently onto her back and kissed his way down the hollow between her breasts. Removing her shirt as he went, revealing her skin inch by inch to be kissed, he trailed his lips over her soft stomach then lower still, feeling her tense in anticipation as he reached the very core of her. He parted her softly with a single stroke of his tongue, then found the swollen nub and drew it into his mouth, sucking gently, feeling every jump and flutter of her muscles as she responded. He slid hands across the warm silk of her skin, wanting her to envelop every one of his senses. Her fingers clutched at his hair as she writhed beneath him and as he pushed her to the edge. He held her hard against his mouth so as to eke out every moment of pleasure.

A brief pause while he reached to the side table for a condom, and then she was moving back against him, circling his rigid erection with one hand and sliding the swollen oversensitised tip against her until a moan escaped his lips.

He found the smooth curve of her bottom with his hand, gripped her in readiness to turn her onto her back so he could fuck her before he lost all threads of control, and then she pre-empted him, moved above him, sliding onto his length, taking him inside her inch by silken inch to the hilt. The sensation was exquisite, taking over his every sense. She'd found a rhythm now, grinding slowly and deliberately against him. He yanked her roughly against him, wanting her skin against his now, wanting that closeness of touch. He found her mouth with his, felt her hard nipples graze his chest, her knees drawn up, all the better to take him in deeper. And still she kept up the delicious grind until he could stand it no longer and in one swift movement he turned her onto her back on the bed.

Tangling one hand in her hair now, he thrust harder, taking her rhythm and increasing the pace as she wrapped her long legs around his back and raised her hips from the bed, pushing himself ever harder into her until he could control it no more and she cried her own ecstasy softly into his hair as he reached the height of his pleasure.

Every second that ticked by was something to treasure.

Her breathing slowly evened, and her body relaxed against his as she melted into sleep. He didn't move, even though he was too hot to sleep, revelling instead in the scent of her hair and her warm breath against his chest. He didn't want to sleep, didn't want to wake up and have just moments left with her. And there it hit him. What the hell was he doing, just accepting her unreasonable terms without question? He'd made that mistake five years ago and really, what did he have to lose by talking to her in the morning, maybe arranging a meeting when he made it back from Barbados?

CHAPTER NINE

'It doesn't need to stop here,' he said.

He leaned up on one elbow, the pillow rucked up beneath his naked chest, dark hair tousled from the night they'd spent tangled together. Golden shards of morning sunlight slipped into the room through the chink in the silk curtains and her stomach churned miserably at the ticking away of minutes until he would be leaving. Part of her wished she'd just left while he slept, like last time. It had been infinitely easier than this.

Her heart gave a tiny leap and she forced it back down. To go along with this would have no better outcome, she'd just be delaying the loss for a few weeks. The moment he was back in the midst of his family with all that history, all that responsibility, she would lose her charm. She didn't fit in with a family. She'd never been able to hold her own with her parents, so why the hell should she assume she'd do better on that front with him? Better to let him go now, no matter that it was a wrench. She'd managed it before and she could do it again.

She smiled.

'Of course it does. It was always going to stop here. Just like it was always going to stop back in Devon. Don't try to make it into something it isn't.'

He sat up in bed next to her.

'I'm not. I'm just asking. Why it has to come to a standstill at all.'

She sighed.

'It is what it is, Tom.'

'And what is that?'

He held her gaze, waited for her answer.

'It's a fling,' she said, slowly, as if explaining to a toddler. 'It's down to circumstance. Five years ago you and I were a spur of the moment one-night stand. It was a fluke. Hotel room. Same place, different time. If you want to pin a name on it, I guess you could call it a holiday romance.'

'And now?'

'Basically the same thing. Same rules, same situation. Both of us are taking time out for a few days from our normal lives – you're stuck here because of the weather and I'm on a shopping break. You and I have never existed in the real world, so what the hell makes you think we could?'

'Fate is on our side.'

She rolled her eyes.

'Will you stop going on about bloody fate? *I* control fate, not the other way around. It's the only way to make sure I don't get kicked in the arse by it.' She sat up in bed herself now, as if warming to her subject. 'Nothing that stands the test of time can be built on such a whim. Think about it. It makes sense really. Two random people brought together by a random situation, who barely even get to know each other beyond a couple of hours' flirting. The chances of them having what it takes to go the distance are miniscule. The whole thing is built on physical attraction, on lust. It isn't the foundation for anything long-lasting. You can't possibly argue anything else. So what I'm saying is that this has been a fantastic couple of days. Just the way it was a fantastic night back then in Devon. But don't pretend it can ever lead to anything more than that. We threw that possibility away at the outset because of the way we got together.'

He bunched fists together with sheer frustration at her smooth, determined, non-emotional bloody certainty.

'You said the chances are miniscule and you might be right, but miniscule allows for the odd exception – right? We could buck the odds.'

He reached for her hand but she gently disentangled her fingers from his.

'I know a hell of a lot about one-night stands and short-term flings,' Ella said. 'I know what I'm talking about.'

The horrified look on his face would have been funny in any other situation.

'Not like that,' she said quickly, shaking her head madly. 'I'm not talking about *me*. I don't actually make a habit of this. You're…'

'What?'

'Well, you're an exceptional case.'

'How so?'

She looked him in the eye.

'I have absolutely no idea. Maybe you're just incredibly persuasive.'

'So if you don't make a habit of this kind of thing, what do you mean, you *know* about it?'

She took a deep breath and looked up at the ceiling with its gleaming chandelier.

'I wasn't talking about me. I was talking about my parents.'

'Your parents?'

She nodded.

'I'm the result of a one-night stand,' she said. 'Some drunken fumble in a dark alleyway outside a nightclub, fuelled entirely by too much alcohol.'

She had no idea of the proper circumstances, had never been able to stomach asking her mother for more details. Just her mother's drunken revelation of the fact itself had been too much information for a fifteen year old girl, without all the surrounding details. But that was how she imagined it had been. Seedy. Not driven by love, or even by proper attraction. Just beer-goggles and lust.

'My mother went ahead with the pregnancy,' she said. 'Obviously.'

'What about your father?'

'They were both teenagers,' she said. 'I saw him on and off for the first few years. They weren't together but he still seemed to make an effort. Maybe that was part of the problem.' She looked down at her hands, thinking back. 'In my head I built him up to be so perfect.' A rueful smile touched the corner of her mouth. 'When he stopped making that effort I made excuses for him. Told myself my mother made it impossible for him to be around. They didn't exactly get on like a house on fire, if you get my drift.'

He smiled at her, but the expression on his face was troubled.

'Anyway, when my mother moved in with Gordy a few years ago I was old enough to make my own choices and I tracked my father down again. I think I expected to be welcomed into his life with open arms. I thought he'd be so pleased to see me again.'

'And how did it go?'

Her stomach churned with the remnants of the awful disappointment she'd felt that day. It was dull now, not sharp and all-consuming as it had been then.

'He was so far from delighted it wasn't even funny,' she said. 'He shut the front door behind him and talked to me on his doorstep, fobbing me off, talking his way out of it. And all the time I stood there I knew it was because he had a proper family behind that front door. He'd never told them about me, I was just a secret, something to be hidden, kept away from his new, perfect life.'

He touched her hand.

'Ella, I'm sorry. That's awful.'

She shook her head furiously.

'Don't apologise. Not for him. I am SO over him. He was a total arse. Why the hell would I want to get to know someone like that? But you understand now, why I walked away without saying goodbye back in Devon. That perfect night could never be the foundation for anything strong or long lasting. You see that, don't you? You can't build a lasting relationship on a one-night stand.'

'But you've gone way beyond that. It's you against the world and no compromise. You'll end up going through life on your own because you're never prepared to let anyone else in.'

'Because I know I can rely on myself. I'm not about to let myself down or disappear out of my own life because I'm too much trouble, am I? What I'm trying to say is that I should never have revisited it. I should never have tracked him down but I did because I believed things could be better second time around. That everything was worth a second chance.'

She looked up at him.

'That's why I was reluctant to speak to you at first, when we bumped into each other again. Not because I didn't want to, or because I regretted what happened between us, but because I didn't want to ruin it. I loved it, every second of it. I didn't want to take the risk of finding out that you weren't all that after all.' She forced a smile up at him. 'As it turned out, you were.'

'I don't care about any of that. When I get back from Barbados, we can get together. Let me show you things can be different for us.'

She sat up in bed and looked into his eyes, saw the determined expression. *When he got back from Barbados.* There was the point, right there. Family first. She could never compete with that, not in the long-term.

Self-preservation won out and she leaned forward to kiss him softly on the mouth.

'You need to get going, Tom. You'll miss your flight.'

***

He was back in the lobby, but checking out this time. Taxi booked, under time pressure now. Had it really only been a couple of days since he'd stood here and she'd teased him for grouching about the snow?

He glanced around the lobby and there was no sign of her. No sign that the weekend had even happened. He should have expected this. She'd made her excuses, left him alone to pack and hadn't reappeared since. Why was he even surprised? After all she'd made it pretty clear that she didn't do goodbyes. This was the way she wanted it, clearly she was able to move forward without looking back. It was a trick he really needed to perfect for himself.

For a moment he wondered if part of the perfection of this was that he knew it wouldn't last? Knew because *she* wouldn't let it. Easy to put things on a pedestal when they weren't subjected to the test of time and daily life. Maybe she was right to let this go – he wasn't happy in his own life, how could he drag her into it and expect her to be happy too?

Then he turned to head for the revolving doors and there she was. Thick sweater, jeans and her hair in soft waves, still lightly damp from the shower. He crossed the lobby toward her, put his bags down next to her. He could pick up the warm citrus scent of the hotel shampoo.

'I thought you were going to skip the goodbyes,' he said.

'Yeah well,' she said, smiling. 'I thought I'd try a different approach this time around.'

He opened his mouth to speak and she stopped it with three fingers.

'Don't,' she said. 'Don't ruin this by trying to make it into more than it can be. Let it be what it is. Let it be that perfect couple of days.'

'That's what you really want?'

Part of him wanted to shake her, talk at her until she gave in. Her infuriating insistence that this was nothing more than a fling. So entrenched in her own way of living that she had no room to consider anything else. No different from the last time. And yet she *had* changed since last time, hadn't she? She'd gone through with the goodbye this time.

'Maybe we're destined to only ever meet by chance,' he said instead. 'Who knows, in five years we might run into each other in the street.'

She smiled into his eyes at that.

'I'll see you in five years then,' she said.

And because his flight was on the brink of leaving, and his responsibilities were well overdue, and because she'd made it crystal clear how this was going to be, he turned and walked toward the waiting taxi.

CHAPTER TEN

She'd got through this once before and she could do it again.

Shopping break weekend over with, Lavington Hotel behind her, and Christmas Day now out of the way. A working Christmas, just like every other year. Card and phone call from her mother but no invitation to visit over the season. As predicted, they were off to Benidorm, which suited Ella perfectly since any moment spent under the same roof as the hideous Gordy would be a moment too many, especially with mistletoe thrown in. Christmas worked perfectly well for her as it was. Triple time on Christmas Day and Boxing Day. Double time for much of the rest of the holiday. The big thaw was well under way now, especially on the coast, and the only evidence that there had ever been a weather front that had thrown her and Tom back together was in the shrinking heaps of greying snow in lay-bys and at the edges of the road where the snowploughs had piled it up. The slushy, miserable aftermath of all that magic. Which was pretty much how it felt when she thought of Tom, and the reason why she was now hurling herself back into work as if her life depended on it.

She'd taken a job this year at the Harbour Hotel in Looe. The first year she'd gone back there since her Gran had died, and she hadn't been sure even as she'd contacted the owner and offered her services, that it would be a good idea. She could earn more working in one of the cities. Yet it seemed easier now, to go back to the tiny coastal town where she'd been so happy for a time. Comforting, rather than painful. Instead of feeling the loss this time she was able to enjoy the icy cold salt air and the Christmas lights strung around the harbour. It occurred to her that maybe that was the key, maybe five years was some kind of a cut off point for getting over things.

If that were the case then she'd just set herself right back to the beginning when it came to Tom.

For Pete's sake, there he was again, drifting through her mind when he was meant to be securely filed away under 'past encounters.'

She would take the wrenching sadness in her chest at the fact it was over because she was the one who'd taken the risk. She'd gone into it with her eyes open. She'd got over him once and so she'd thought he hadn't been all that, had believed she could take the fun from the encounter and not get stung by the aftermath.

She'd been wrong.

She knew now she'd never really got over him, had never really moved on. Who had she been close to since? Liz? A couple of other girlfriends? No man had moved her in the way he had. And she had no one to blame but herself. She'd flouted her no-second-time rule at her peril, and there was nothing to do now except get on with things.

She should never have broken that rule, but at least she'd pulled things around before they went any further. A clean break, that was the best policy. Because if it hurt now, how much worse would it be if she'd let it go further? She dreaded to think, because it felt pretty damn crushing now thank you very much.

***

A tiny, skinny cliff road covered with sheet ice; he must be totally nuts.

Tom Henley shifted gear down yet again and concentrated hard on seeing further ahead than the ten or so feet the coastal fog and his dipped headlights allowed. No time for reckless driving now. He hadn't spent Christmas rejigging his responsibilities and making sacrifices only to zip off the edge of a cliff before he could even find her. And of course the biggest hurdle still lay ahead. Her stubbornness scared him far more than a bit of sea-fog and ice.

The road began to descend and as he drove through the town centre, heading for the seafront, the mist thinning enough for him to pick out the coloured Christmas lights on houses lining the harbour.

Knowing the name of the town was one thing of course, finding the bloody restaurant was another, but of course he was helped by the fact her grandmother had lived here. Local people would know Ella, might be able to point him in the right direction. He struck lucky in the fourth pub, where the landlord knew Ella. From there it was just a short walk. The air was crystal clear and he could taste the salt in it as he walked.

The Harbour Hotel had steamy windows and a low-beamed rustic bar that ran the length of the building, mismatched furniture and a live band playing loud jaunty music. With it being New Years Eve, the bar was packed to the rafters and you couldn't have shoehorned in another reveller if you'd tried. He shouldered his way to the bar and ordered a beer.

Minutes ticked by, enough for him to wonder if he'd got the right place after all, and then suddenly there she was. Black skinny trousers, white shirt, tray of drinks held at shoulder height and a look of disbelief on her face.

'Happy New Year,' he said.

***

With her tray of drinks delivered, she nodded her head toward the outer lobby of the hotel, where it was possible to actually hear yourself think.

'It hasn't been five years,' she said, turning around and looking up at him, eyes wide.

'I know,' he said, drinking her in with his eyes. 'It's been ten days.' She looked tired. For Pete's sake, she'd probably worked all the hours she could over the festive season and she was clearly run off her feet. Her way of avoiding the fact that she was celebrating Christmas and New Year all on her own. He felt the desperate urge to take her away from that grind, look after her, give her some of the support she lacked.

'Long enough for me to know I don't want it ever to be any longer than that,' he said. 'Long enough for me to check on my father and talk to both my parents.'

'About?'

'My life, what I want from it. A way of maybe achieving that without letting them down.' He shrugged. 'A compromise.'

'And?'

He looked away briefly, she saw the guilt flash across his face.

'My father was disappointed. Of course he was, I always knew he would be. He was pretty low on the first day but I think he's coming round to it now. He told me it did worry him, me taking on all that responsibility so young – he didn't join the practice himself until he was nearly forty. He'd spent time as an army doctor, you see. In a way, he knew exactly where I was coming from all along. If I'd only confided in him earlier instead of keeping quiet for fear of upsetting him, things could have been very different.'

'So what about joining the practice? I thought you were going to take over in the New Year. That's tomorrow.'

'I'll still need to take a background role in the management. We'll take on an extra partner and I'll take some blocks of time out to do some charity trips.' He shrugged. 'It'll take some time to organise but I'll get there.' He held her gaze steadily with his own. 'So then there's just you and me to sort out.'

Her heart was pounding in her chest as he took her hand.

'I want us to be together, Ella. Yes, I'll be away on the occasional trip, but I'll be based here. You can build up your business, we can move forward and have a future together.' He paused. 'Unless I'm not really what you want. If you still want to walk away, say so now and I'll leave you in peace. Your obsession with the perfect night, the perfect fling, your determination never to revisit the past. How can you ever expect to make something work in the long-term if you can't face seeing how it will work outside that bubble? We're strong enough for that, Ella, I really think we are, but we won't know until we try.'

'Did you really think I walked away either time because of some shortfall of *yours*?' She couldn't keep back a mirthless laugh. 'For Pete's sake, could you *be* any more perfect? You were a doctor, you had the world at your feet, a close family who loved you and a fabulous supportive upbringing. I knew I'd never measure up. I could never fit in your life, even just the tiny bit of it that I knew about told me that. And I'd been left behind so many times, Tom. I didn't want to be left behind by you.'

His heart turned achingly over in his chest as he looked at her.

'Your family background couldn't be more different to mine. My parents were never there for me. The only person who really ever fought my corner was my Gran, and I lost her too. I couldn't face dealing with that again so I kept people at a distance. I decided I'd make my own security in life, without having to rely on anyone else. But it was so hard at first.

'That first night I spent with you was the first time since Gran died that I actually felt like I could be happy, like I could turn things around. I looked at you with your life mapped out and your big dreams and I knew I might not have your support network and cheerleading family but I was still determined to make something of my life, for me. Not for anyone else.'

She shrugged.

'I thought by leaving early I'd get in first. If I'd stayed in bed with you that morning I knew exactly what I was in for. We would have spent an hour or two together, we would have had coffee, maybe in that little beach café where they gave you free top-ups and you could watch the tide come in and still be warm. We would have made awkward small talk because both of us knew our time was up. And then it would have been time for you to go and drive to the airport, catch your flight. We would have said our goodbyes and that would be an end to it. And when it came right down to it I just couldn't face that. I decided to get in first – I somehow thought it would be easier if I could make it my decision.' She shrugged. What it comes down to is that it would have ended anyway last time around. You would still have said goodbye if I'd hung around to hear it. I just didn't give you the chance.'

'That's where you're wrong,' he said. 'I was going to suggest we stay in touch.'

Her heart lurched.

'Yeah, yeah, you say that now—'

'It's true,' he said, and held both hands up at her cynical expression. 'Just for the record… I wasn't going to just leave.'

'Even if you hadn't,' she said. 'It would never have lasted. Nothing's changed, Tom. I told you my views. Nothing long-term can come from something that's grounded on sex. However hot the sex,' she added.

'I know,' he said. 'I've got a loophole for that.' His grin was triumphant, as if he'd been expecting this from her. 'We're up to two now with our flings. How many do you reckon we need to have before we become grounded in something more than just sex?'

She was shaking her head at him like she thought he might have lost his mind.

'I think we should have another fling. Right now. To take us over New Year. Then we'll see what we both want to do – where we want to go, what our commitments are – and we'll schedule another one. I'll book the hotel, you meet me there. I reckon half a dozen might do it. By then I'll have you paring down your luggage, and maybe I will have met some of your friends. We won't be the one-night stand couple anymore. Our lives will start to overlap more and more and we'll have a *foundation*. We can build a future on one of those.'

Quiet tendrils of hope began to course their way through her body. He'd come back. Christmas in Barbados hadn't been enough of a pull to keep him through to New Year.

He tapped his head.

'It's mind over matter. You're determined to view us as having no chance because you equate our relationship to your parents. That's really unfair to us. We were lucky enough to have fate bring us back together and...'

'Will you please stop bringing bloody fate into it!' she said, exasperated. 'Fate hasn't been kind to me over the years.'

'That's exactly my point,' he said, pulling her into a cuddle. 'I think fate owes you one. Maybe it's time we took charge of it.'

She let her arms slide around his neck. He had an answer for every damn reservation. Whispers of tentative excitement began to spread through her as she tested the idea in her mind. She, Ella Scott, was thinking long-term and including someone else in those plans. It felt totally alien and at the same time intoxicating.

Somewhere in the background the countdown to midnight began, with more and more voices chiming in. And then he was kissing her, his arm around her waist, his hand tangling in her hair.

New Year. New beginnings. Second chances.

She gave fate a chance and kissed him back.